BEST CANADIAN STORIES
2023

BEST
CANADIAN
STORIES

2023

EDITED BY

MARK ANTHONY JARMAN

BIBLIOASIS

WINDSOR, ONTARIO

FIRST EDITION
ISBN 978-1-77196-501-9 (Trade Paper)
ISBN 978-1-77196-502-6 (eBook)

Edited by Mark Anthony Jarman
Copyedited by Chandra Wohleber
Cover and text designed by Gordon Robertson

 Canada Council
for the Arts
Conseil des Arts
du Canada

 ONTARIO ONTARIO
CREATES CRÉATIF

 ONTARIO ARTS COUNCIL
CONSEIL DES ARTS DE L'ONTARIO
an Ontario government agency
un organisme du gouvernement de l'Ontario

Published with the generous assistance of the Canada Council for the Arts,
which last year invested $153 million to bring the arts to Canadians throughout
the country, and the financial support of the Government of Canada. Biblioasis
also acknowledges the support of the Ontario Arts Council (OAC), an agency
of the Government of Ontario, which last year funded 1,709 individual artists
and 1,078 organizations in 204 communities across Ontario, for a total of
$52.1 million, and the contribution of the Government of Ontario through
the Ontario Book Publishing Tax Credit and Ontario Creates.

PRINTED AND BOUND IN CANADA

CONTENTS

INTRODUCTION
Mark Anthony Jarman

This collection is a tribute to the talent of Steven Heighton, who died earlier this year. His death was a profound shock to me. In April I emailed Steve to tell him I was taking his story "Instructions for the Drowning" for this book. I had no idea he was in the hospital. He wrote, "Thank you for choosing the story, which Metcalf adores. I hoped you would too. I wish I could have been with you on your walk and for that beer. Maybe on the other side of this."

Steve kept his illness quiet. In March I was in Marseille and emailed him a link to an article on refugees, a topic close to his heart; he sent "slightly envious good wishes" of our stay in Marseille. He had to be very sick at that point, but made no mention of health problems.

That April email I sent Steve about his story was on a Saturday. On Tuesday I heard that he was dead. It was stunningly fast, seventy-two hours. I'm glad I sent that email when I did.

In his honour we are also including a second Heighton piece that I had my eye on, "Everything Turns Away." I hope all the other talented writers in this stellar volume are honoured to be in this, a commemorative issue, a sad occasion, but also a community celebration of scribes and friends. As

Miriam Toews said recently in *The Walrus*, "Writing is an act of friendship, of reaching out and feeling less alone."

The works gathered in this year's *Best Canadian Stories* are drawn from all over the world: there are tales of Balkan musicians in Toronto and lost coffee plantations in French Indochina, strange gambling halls in the American West, the curse of fossil fuels, and the back seat of a police cruiser. Carmelinda Scian's evocative story is set in Portugal, but it was published in Hong Kong. For better or worse, we're global. Some of these writers I was aware of: Omar El Akkad, Caroline Adderson, Tamas Dobozy, David Bezmozgis, Jowita Bydlowska, David Huebert, Kate Cayley. Other names are newer, but very good to know: Philip Huynh, Naomi Fontaine, Sara Freeman, Christine Estima, Alexandra Mae Jones; all are welcome in these pages, under this improvised roof.

I'd like to thank the magazine editors who worked with these writers. Thanks also to Dan Wells and the dedicated staff at Biblioasis for their help with this project, and a belated thank-you to John Metcalf for introducing me to Steven way back at the Wild Writers conference in 2000, a fun gathering where John hoped younger writers might forge lifelong connections.

Thanks to the writers and thanks as well to the readers, who are crucial to all of this. As John Cheever said, "I can't write without a reader. It's precisely like a kiss—you can't do it alone."

INSTRUCTIONS FOR THE DROWNING

Steven Heighton

Ray's father once told him that if you ever jumped into the water to help a drowning man, he would try to pull you down with him and there was only one way to save yourself and him as well. Drowning men were men possessed and they were supernaturally strong. But they were also as weak as babies, seeing as they had lost all self-control.

His father shook his head, his lips clamped thin, as if such a loss were the most pitiful any man might suffer. You could neither wrestle nor reason with a man in that condition, he explained. In a sense, he was hardly human anymore.

Ray—ten or eleven years old—had pictured the victim metamorphosing into a kind of ghoul, sinewy and slippery as the Gollum he had been imagining while reading *The Lord of the Rings*.

So you would have no choice, his father concluded, his eyes narrowing and hardening behind the steel-rimmed spectacles, a gaze that always preceded a briefing on some unfortunate but unavoidable masculine duty. A drowning man would have to be knocked out cold. For his own good. A short, clean punch to the side of the jaw—that would be the preferred blow. After which you could easily complete the rescue, towing the victim in to shore. (In the boy's adaptation, the victim was tamed from raving fiend to serenely compliant human, slightly smiling, eyes closed, like those cartoon characters who always looked so gratified to have been knocked out.)

How rescuers who were not world-class water polo players were to find the leverage and stability to land a decisive blow while being dragged underwater by a panicking man was not a question the boy could have formed or would have posed. If his father said the operation worked—and he made it sound like one performed routinely in the summer lakes of Canada and the northern states—then it must.

Over the years Ray would hear other men, usually older, mention the technique often enough to gather that it had once been endorsed, if not actually practised, by a whole generation. Now it seems as dubious and dated as the quaint medical certainties of another age. Yet this afternoon, as Ray's wife, Inge, floating near the end of the dock, cries out and begins splashing and coughing, it's not the sensible modern rules of aquatic rescue that first leap to mind but his old man's advice. Then comes the thought that he's not even sure what the modern rules are. He springs up out of the fold-out recliner and pulls off his sunglasses, his latest can of IPA tipping and rolling off the dock. The blood drains from his head—he is almost drunk, he was almost asleep—and the glasses slip from his hand as he stands swaying. His sight returns. There's Inge, treading water effortlessly, using just one arm. Her sunlit face is strained. Another cough hacks out of her, but then she calls hoarsely, "It's okay—okay!"

"What? You sure?"

"Just a cramp. My leg. But I think it's ..."

"Inge?"

She winces, her teeth white in the sun. From the other direction, behind Ray, a jocular voice calls down, "Hey, you two lovebirds all right down there?"

"Okay!" he shouts back automatically toward the cottage, where their hosts, Hugh and Alison, have retired for a little nap, as Hugh always puts it. Hugh and Alie enjoy a spirited, irreverent rapport, playfully and publicly physical. In the penumbra around them, other couples in their circle are never quite free of a sense of deficiency and demotion.

With a choked groan Inge vanishes as if something has yanked her feet from below. She flails back up, arms flapping and reaching. She could be a woman playing the victim during a lifeguard training session or someone just gauchely fooling around. No. She is a decent swimmer and she is no joker; she laughs readily enough with her friends and with Ray, even these days, but she dislikes physical comedy and April Fool's pranks of the kind that Hugh loves to devise.

Ray charges down the dock and jumps off the end where a half-empty wineglass perches as if on the edge of a bar. The water here is deep, but he dives flatly, smacking his paunch and his groin and surfacing fast. He is an ugly swimmer, a heaver and splasher, his head always turtled above the water— he hates submerging his face—but he is strong, and padded enough that he floats.

All that's visible of Inge is her face tipped sunward like a tiny, shrinking island. He calls, "Hang on!" and she stammers back, "Help, help, help me now, Ray!" It's a shock to hear *help* used right on cue and exactly as it should be. And her accent— for as long as they have known each other it has been faint, but for rare spasms of anger or passion. Now it's thickly Dutch. Her face dips under, comes back up, her mouth gawping, hands flogging the water. "I'm here," he says, and extends his left hand. "Inge?" She launches toward him. Her facial muscles flex and contort and he gets a flashback of that gurning creature conjured up by his father's words some thirty years ago. Her eyes—pure blue, no pupil—do seem half-alien, perceiving but not knowing him.

She hugs and envelops him, the way she might an exciting new man, as perhaps she already has, who can say? They've been sleeping separately for almost a year, although not on this visit, and the bed-sharing up here is not merely for show or to pre-empt gossip—and Hugh and Alie are gossips—no, they really are trying to give it one more shot, and the sex last night was good, partly because it had been a while and partly because of the fresh setting and the voluptuous breezes floating in, and also, sure, because they both knew without saying a word that they would team up and show Hugh and Alie, ostentatiously coupling in the next room, that they too had a marriage.

Her skin last night was hot as always, much hotter than his. Her crushing embrace now is icy. She's all over him, clinging to him like the one thing afloat on an empty sea. *Grasping at straws.* Now he gets it. It's not about drawing lots but about grabbing handfuls of the useless stuff floating up from the hold of a sinking ship.

She's pulling him down. Grappling—*Inge, don't!*—an arm, trying to wrench free. Impossible, just like his father said. His eyes are above the water, then below: a glimpse of locked, thrashing forms, bubbles swarming, her skinny white legs hooked around his waist.

They surface. He inhales a breath, she choking and gasping. Somehow he's facing the shore. Hugh and Alie, in the matching aqua sarongs from their March holiday in Goa, are running down the flagstone steps from the cottage. Inge is climbing Ray as if he's a dockside ladder—his knees, his thighs, his shoulders the rungs. Kicking her way up she forces him down. Water floods his yelling mouth and he gags, digs her clawing grip off his shoulder, fends her off with both hands, flattening her breasts under the one-piece she always wears up here because of Alie, who makes her untypically shy, *Nice,* she says, *I get the pot-belly but not the baby,* though it's not really much of a belly, not compared with his. She surges toward him again. He parries her arms but her legs pincer around his hips with fantastic strength and she pulls him back down. *You're going to kill us both! Inge!* Her face underwater is deathly pale and yet frantically alive, wild eyes unseeing, hair billowing. He grabs at the surface, the light, somehow drags them both back up. He spews out water and gasps. Without thinking or revisiting his father's crazy advice, he hits her.

The blow misses the jaw—*the jaw*, as if it's any old jaw, not Inge's jaw—and grazes her cheek. Her eyes open even wider. He has never hit her—though a few times recently her charged silence made him wonder if he would have to duck a punch of hers. He has never punched anyone, not since grade school. He forgets whatever technical instruction his father once gave him. Her legs pincer tighter. Feet scrabbling for traction, he swings again. At the same time she jerks her head sideways, toward the blow, reinforcing it. Fist and jaw meet with a crack and her eyes roll upward. Her leg-grip slackens, her whole body sags. Panting, spitting, he half turns and cradles her torso with his left arm, scooping at the water with his right. "It's okay. I'll get us back. I'm sorry. Hang on." He frog-kicks, hindered by her dragging legs, aiming for the dock where Hugh and Alie now loom, leaning forward, hollering like swim coaches exhorting their athletes on the home stretch.

Inge tenses, twitches as if snapping out of a doze. He looks at her face on his shoulder. Her reopened eyes focus. Her fist leaps out of the water like a fish and she clouts him square in the nose, slipping under after she connects. "Jesus, Inge!" His eyes, already blurred, tear up from the punch. He twists free of her. Hugh and Alie stand staring, hands lax at their sides, as if it's occurring to them that maybe no one is drowning here, maybe Ray and Inge are just having a fight—a real, physical fight, not like a professional couple on a long-weekend getaway but like a pair of locals, those trailer park townies whose bonfire parties at the public beach down the shore so obviously test Hugh and Alie's liberal tolerance . . . All of this

7

he absorbs in a moment as he opens his mouth to call out—
but then Inge jumps him from behind and hauls him back
under. He tears at the pale, magnified hands clamping his rib
cage, the rigid fingers with their bitten nails. Around them
the water grows darker, colder. Bubbles boil upward in silence,
lighting a route back to the surface. Suddenly, already, it looks
too far. He could surrender, he could just inhale, it would be
less painful, painless, he has heard, but he rips himself free as
if from a jammed seat belt in a sinking car and shoots upward.

Sunlight detonates. His lungs erupt, shooting out water,
blood as well, his nostrils hot with blood, his eyes half-blind.
She pops up beside him, gagging and coughing. She throws
another, limper punch but misses. He is breathing ammonia,
briny mucus. She rears toward him again as if to attack, but
no, she is churning, sputtering past him on the right, toward
the dock, seemingly restored by her rage. He's furious himself
now. Alie is calling in a thick and breaking voice, "It's all right,
you two. Don't worry. Come on. Just come in!"

Ray keeps coughing, though weakly. He's still in trouble,
in fact, and could probably do with a little help himself. Hugh
is tearing off his sarong, crouching, flicking it out so that one
end trails in the water like a rope, a few strokes short of Inge's
reach as she labours toward the dock. Hugh should be naked
now but isn't. (Is that underwear?) Beside his splayed feet,
Inge's wineglass still stands. Alie is poised to dive in but Hugh
cups a hand over her kneecap; Inge is managing just enough
not to need rescuing. "It's okay, girl!" Alie says, kneeling down
beside Hugh, her voice throbbing, "You're there!"

Ray's legs feel heavy as anchors and his pummelling heart
skips beats as he side-strokes toward the dock, toward Inge,
who now grabs the floating end of the sarong with both hands.
Hugh stands up—he actually is wearing underwear, baggy
white boxers—and tows her in. She glances back at Ray. Her
stricken gaze might be fixed on a dangerous pursuer or, yearn-
ingly, a loved one falling behind in the course of some desper-

ate escape. One of her hands releases the taut sarong as if she means to point, wave, beckon. Alie grabs the free hand and tugs upward; Hugh reaches down as well; Inge is suspended off the end of the dock, continuing to gaze back at him.

It occurred to him later that the crisis, from the moment he realized she was in trouble until he himself was dragged up onto the dock, could not have taken more than three minutes. A few hundred heartbeats. It felt interminable, of course. His memories—resolving into vivid fragments, like violent few-second cellphone videos posted on a news site—felt hyper-real and indelibly stable, as if exempt from memory's normal fading and smudging.

But he could not test their accuracy by discussing them with Inge. Her refusal to revisit the crisis—their near deaths, their mutual violence, her once-in-a-lifetime relinquishing of all self-control—was hardly surprising, especially given what they learned soon afterward. Still, in spite of everything, she surprised him the following year by wanting to return to the lake for their customary long-weekend stay. Hugh, he warned her, would certainly try to discuss the incident and his and Alie's own role in it. But Inge was adamant. She seemed to view the return not so much as a form of trauma exorcism but rather as a way of salvaging an important tradition, in a matured familial form. She meant to swim as much as ever (though in the end, as it turned out, she chose not to go back in at all). As for Hugh and Alie, she realized they could be annoyingly self-satisfied, but they were true friends and that mattered more than ever now.

For the first five years of their marriage, Inge and Ray had tried to have a baby, suffered miscarriages, consulted specialists, and in due course accepted that there would be no children. No way to know if children would have prevented or accelerated the fraying of their marriage over the following three years, leading up to that struggle in the lake. But a few weeks after it, trying to work out the details of a separation, they discovered Inge was pregnant. At first, pending the re-test, she was tense, touchy, guarded, as if she dreaded either outcome; with the second positive, an unqualified joy overcame her, an *exultancy* that seemed to astonish her as much as her condition. Ray, his two black eyes now faded to yellow, felt himself bumped into the role of designated worrier, the sober, tentative one, although he too felt more pleased by the surprise than he would have predicted. That the summer's lone interlude of carnality, however mutually satisfying, had resulted in conception—a result supposedly impossible—made him wonder, ever so slightly, if Hugh could have been responsible.

The boy was born in April. He could not have looked more like Ray. At the cottage in August, their first afternoon, after Hugh and Alie had retired for their nap, Inge, on the dock, unwrapped Isaac and handed him down to Ray, who was standing in the shallows by the tiny beach.

"Inge, are you sure?"

"Don't be silly, Ray. Go on, let him get the feel of it."

Ray held his naked son so that the boy faced away from him, out over the lake, Ray's hands all but encircling the rib cage and feeling the thudding of the tiny heart. He dunked him to his navel. Isaac's pale legs began frogging promisingly, his whole body writhing as if longing to be released.

ALL OUR AULD ACQUAINTANCES ARE GONE

Caroline Adderson

Only about half the apartments were lit and fewer had Christmas lights, just like the last building. They must have walked around the block and ended up back at the same glassy, germless place. Even the Christmas tree in the white marble lobby was a twin, like it had come ready-decorated out of the box.

She asked Cory, "Weren't we just here?"

He'd found cigarettes and a lighter in the coat pocket. When he answered smoke hung on his words, or the cold wrote them in the air.

"That was back by where we parked. Same builder probably. Half these condos are empty. They're investments."

He'd worked in construction, so she believed him, just like she'd believed when he'd said one party. Somebody had told him about it and she went along. Then, when they were leaving, walking all natural down the hall to the elevator in their new coats and shoes, they passed an open door where another party was happening. The loud music sucked Cory in.

Nobody spoke to her at the first party, but at the second this dude with sideburns came over and asked, "And what are you going to do to make your pretty little life sparkle in 2020?"

Now here they were when they should have been driving, but Cory was on a roll, going for three times lucky, whatever that meant. She'd never known it even once. An ache kicked her in different places. Behind one eye.

"What time is it?" she asked.

He hiked the coat up at the back to get at his phone. "Eleven sixteen."

"I'm feeling like Cinderella here."

"I know."

"So let's go. We're good now."

"How're those shoes?"

She looked down at them. They'd picked a shadow to wait in, a spot between the streetlight and the light pouring out of the glassed-in lobby. Darkness drained the crayon colour from the shoes. Green with purple piping, buckles.

"I feel stupid."

"Be careful how you walk. Don't do that thing."

"What thing?"

"Half the time you look about to fall over."

This made her want to sit down. She went over to the planter and sank her ass onto the cold cement. She'd left the last place with one of those shiny gift bags with string handles. It clinked when she set it on the ground.

"Feel this." Cory held out his arm. "It's cashmere."

Meaning expensive. It suited him with his new haircut. The first few days without his dirty yellow ponytail, she'd kept forgetting. She'd be waiting some place and this dude would come along. He would only be Cory when he smiled. Or Kayla would nudge her. Kayla always knew him right away, would twist her hair around one finger and sigh. She thought Cory was *sooo* hot.

Two men walked past, one in a ski jacket, the other an overcoat, tall and short. Then a car drove by so slowly it was impossible not to feel watched. Looking for parking, it turned out. Cold in the thin raincoat, she curled over and hugged herself. Her gaze met the wine. At least she'd thought it was wine when she grabbed the bag off the table, but only now did she reach inside.

Wine. There was a card, too, which she drew out and opened. An angel on one knee, like it was proposing. She tossed it into the planter behind her just as her leg spasmed.

"Cramp?" he asked.

She nodded, one foot off the ground, leg stretched out like she was admiring the gay-ass shoe. "You?"

"I'm fine. I'm pumped."

The fingers of pain slowly released. *I'm not doing this.* She opened her mouth to say it, but just then a couple turned off the sidewalk and started walking toward them. Cory nodded as they passed.

He switched to his animal mode then, eyes focused on some point in the distance. He wasn't seeing anything. He was listening to the beeping as the couple punched a number into the building's intercom, then its amplified ringing. At precisely the right moment he made a dart of the cigarette and headed for the door. She picked up the wine and followed, lurching on the shoes.

The door buzzed. The dude, Indian or something, held it open for his white girlfriend. Cory came up fast behind them. "Going to the party?"

Dude hesitated, still holding the door. He had a goatee and a diamond stud in one ear. "Joe and Perry's?"

"Yeah." Cory smiled without the missing tooth. Farther back in his mouth, it only showed when he smiled for real. "But we can get buzzed in, no problem. We were just having a smoke before going up."

Dude flicked his eyes over them, stopping on the gift bag hanging on her arm. His girlfriend was already in the lobby, their own wine jutting from her oversized handbag, just the neck of it, a twist of brown paper. Shrugging, he let go of the door.

Cory caught it and kept two steps behind. She tripped along after them, heart having a fit now that they were inside.

At the elevator Cory lunged for the Up button. That way Dude would press the button for the floor. At least that was what happened last time. While they waited, they looked in four directions—at the white-baubled tree in the corner, the lobby's white walls screaming for a spray can, the numbers lighting up then dying with the elevator's descent. The girlfriend inspected her perfect nails. The elevator came and they stepped inside. Sure enough, Dude punched twenty-four.

She kept her eyes on the floor numbers lighting as they climbed. The weightless sensation should have cancelled out the dread. Dude's spicy aftershave didn't help. She put her hand on her stomach, feeling through the coat for the rectangular comfort of her phone.

At floor twelve Dude broke the silence. "So are you a lawyer too?"

His girlfriend nudged him. She had long, stiff blond hair and makeup that looked like it might flake off.

"Oh, right. That's an inappropriate question. What can I ask him, hon?"

"For one, you could have asked if *she* was a lawyer."

An exhalation of scorn escaped her, though no one seemed to hear it.

Cory said, "Ask my favourite cereal then."

"No. Let me guess it. You're a muesli man, am I right?"

The woman rolled her eyes. "I'm Michelle. He's Raj." She gave him a jab, which he pretended in an actorly way hurt.

"I'm Scott," Cory said.

She blanked on the name they'd decided for her this time. Different name, different coat, different shoes, different hair. Different people in the security video in the identical lobbies. But the name was gone, like Kayla. Where was she? Muesli was porridge, sort of. Breakfast was a half-finished Starbucks drink fished out of the trash. Or did he have muesli this morning *at his mom's*?

They were looking at her, waiting.

"I'm Angel." It just popped into her head.

Cory stiffened beside her.

"I love your shoes," Michelle said. "Are they Fluevogs?"

The elevator pinged and opened. Raj stepped out first. "See, I would find that an inappropriate question. What if she got them at Walmart?"

Michelle shook her head. "I don't think so."

"What if I stole them?" she said, and they all laughed.

The four of them headed down the hall, Cory squeezing her shoulder, holding her back. *WTF?* it meant. They could hear the party up ahead, the throb of music, shout-talking. A tingling broke out across her face. She lifted her shoulder and tried to shake Cory off.

They both started to slow as they neared the party. The smaller gestures, like pressing the Up button first, like going ahead as if they knew the way—they'd talked about this. It bolstered their cred. But now Cory was squeezing. *Don't act like a nutcase, babe.* If they'd been walking in front they would have blown it because Raj and Michelle sailed right past the party door. So they did too.

She shot Cory a triumphant look. He loosened his grip. Patted her back.

"We can drop in there if Joe's sucks," Raj said.

"This is our third party. We aren't staying long." She said it to Cory.

"Popular," Raj said. "It's our first."

"We had dinner with my mom," Michelle explained.

Joe and Perry's was just two doors along, same side. Raj knocked pointlessly before opening the door and nearly hitting somebody standing just inside. Techno music poured out. He and Michelle went in sideways.

Now she said it, what she'd wanted to tell Cory out front. "I can't. Give me some money."

"In and out, like you said."

"I mean *at all*. I can't do *any* of it. I don't *want to*."

Cory took her face in his hands—clean now, even his nails—but still textured from the street. Forehead pressed against hers, eyes an inch away, he drove his resolve right into her. "Yes, you can ... Angel."

Hand on her back, he guided her inside.

Michelle had taken off her coat, exposing a meaty nylon bulge of thigh between her boot tops and skirt. She was staring at the footwear piled around the door.

"Do we have to take off our shoes? It ruins your outfit."

"I'm having sock insecurity," Raj said.

Michelle said to her, "You're not taking yours off, are you?"

She pointed to the people lingering at the end of the hall. Some were wearing shoes. Michelle smiled and, passing Raj her coat, strode off in her boots. Raj frowned at the hooks that lined the wall, already layered with coats. No vacancy in the closet either.

A woman in a fringed wrap stepped out of the room off the hall. "They're putting them on the bed now," she said. Raj ducked in with their coats, then out again empty-handed. With a wave to them, he went after Michelle, disappearing into the crowded main room.

She took off the raincoat. Under it, a short black dress with complicated sleeves, hardly sleeves at all, sheer nylon stitched to the thicker fabric of the dress. Below the elbow they flared so if she held her arms out at her sides that part of the sleeve hung down like wings. She'd got it for the kangaroo pocket, to carry her phone. Boxing Week at Winners. The harried clerks, past the point of caring, only counted the hangers before handing over the numbered plastic disc that supposedly matched the clothes you were trying on. Anybody can take off a security tag with a hair elastic. Kayla had taught her. Three Kaylas in the wings of the change room mirror, ball cap and bra, ink flowers twining up her arms. They'd made each other friendship bracelets like they were eight or something. Their names made them sound like sisters. She wound the elastic the way Kayla showed her. The tag popped right off and Kayla smiled her own broken smile.

Cory was having trouble giving up his coat. Before handing it over, he held it by the collar and brushed at some unseeable speck. He showed her the label sewn inside. "See? Cashmere." Draping it across her waiting arms, he said, "Goodbye."

"I'll be fast," she said. "Don't go away."

"I'm talking to the coat."

She stepped into the room, closing the door just enough that the music receded to a pulse. All the way would look suspicious, though she was less nervous about getting caught now than anxious to get it done. The only light was a lamp on the bedside table draped with some kind of cloth, as though to dim the room even more. Gradually, she made out a pile of coats on the bed, tossed theirs into it, then craned to see into the space next to the wall where the purses were stashed. She added the bag with the wine.

The first curdling wave hit her then. She shut her eyes and swayed, her hand pressing her phone, on fire and drenched at the same time. A blunt, bitter stab against the back of her throat—just a hint of what was coming. All of this was pointless. No way could she do it. Maybe Cory could. He hadn't been around that long. Also, something was waiting for him on the other side, in that other life where she wasn't welcome. She'd gone and seen it that afternoon, taken the SkyTrain all the way out in her winged dress, soared over the different-coloured roofs and shiny toy cars parked along the streets. His mother said he could move back in if he cleaned up. But not her. He'd been there two nights, had snuck her in so they could get ready for tonight.

"Holy, look at you," he'd said.

His mother's heavy tread crossed the low ceiling. Just a shitty bungalow with a basement suite that stank of bleach. But compared to the underpass? Or the tarp they'd rigged up over two carts until one of them got jacked? Last night, while Cory slept in his boyhood home, she went off with some dude who said they could crash where they impounded the cars. In the morning, she woke alone to crows croaking and rattling, condensation all over the windows, a silver nest made of her own breath. Her pants tossed onto the hood of the car, soaked with rain. She couldn't remember a thing about how they got there. She missed Kayla so bad then.

The wave passed. She rubbed her arms through the sleeves. Something prickled the back of her neck—not sweat. Not a symptom. An instinct, or some higher numbered sense. Somebody's eyes boring into her. She thought of Kayla's eyes, the way they rolled back to show the red stitching of veins. Kayla splayed out on the ground, her cap three feet away. *But where did they take her?* she'd asked Cory. Where do you go after that?

Cory didn't know. All he'd said was *We're getting out of here.*

Somebody was in the room. She swung round, saw a bulky shape filling the chair in the corner.

"God! You scared me!"

"Sorry." It was a woman, half whispering.

"I was just wondering if it was safe to leave my purse."

Why had she made an excuse before she was accused of anything? She could have told the truth, that she'd stood there so long because she felt sick. She was out of the habit. True things sounded like lies. She didn't even have a purse.

Again that hushed voice. "Stick it under there." The woman pointed at something with her stockinged foot.

She came closer. On the other side of the bed was a portable crib. She looked directly at the woman then, first at her face in the shadows—dark hair, long nose. Then her bulkiness transformed to include the blanket draped over her shoulder and around the baby. A little toque perched on its head.

Who would bring a baby to a loud party? It didn't seem that different from pushing a stroller down the alley looking to score—something she disapproved of too, though it was better than being passed from one non-mother to the next with your whole life stuffed in a garbage bag.

"I'll just stick it in my coat," she said, taking a step back.

She flitted her eyes around the room, trying to think of something normal to say before getting away. It didn't seem that dark now. Curtains, furniture—all revealed. The bass in the music made the picture above the woman's head vibrate against the wall like nervous teeth. She felt so bad for the baby.

"How old?"

"Three months," the woman said. "Which is about the last time I slept. He has no trouble sleeping of course. Unless I do. Then he immediately wakes up. They're funny things."

A bell tinkled in her pocket. She took the phone out and gestured toward the door with it.

The woman said, "Would you do me a favour? Bring me something to eat? I sent my husband, but he's gone AWOL."

"Sure."

"Thanks!"

She stepped into the hall. Cory had already hung up, but was texting now.

How's it going
Somebody's in ther wher r you
Balcony

He was supposed to be watching the hall. She thumbed in *??? Let's go*
1 sec

Water trickled out of her nose. She pressed it with the back of her hand. Cory had the money and the cards. Otherwise she'd leave right now.

Another cramp. She braced against the wall to stretch it out. The coats hung there two or three deep, pockets begging to be searched. But there were people steps away at the end of the hall. They'd only have to turn their heads.

She tested the leg then walked straight into the party in the teetering way Cory apparently hated.

There was a fireplace at one end of the room, an open kitchen at the other. Square furniture that nobody sat on. People stood in pairs or tight groups, elbow to elbow, talking loudly over the music. She cut through their groupings. Nobody looked at her.

A long table of food. She lifted the tongs and started loading a plate for the woman with the baby, thinking of cardboard. Cardboard flattened on the sidewalk. A smorgasbord of things you can eat mixed up with things you can't. Jars of No Name p.b., mission sandwiches, binned and stolen crap. Broken phones, granola bars, Percocet. She piled cubes and rolls on the plate. What half of it was, she didn't know. It looked like it would come back up whole.

Beyond the glass wall was a balcony almost as large as the inside space, and as crowded. Finally, she spotted him. With his bony face, he looked like a fake-junkie model in his new mother-bought clothes. He was talking to a man in a suit with a shaved head, touching his arm, for sure calling him *Bro*. It bugged her when he did that. Why? He *was* a brother. He came from an actual family. He could go live in Mommy's basement, *but not her*.

Those condemning footfalls.

She'd hardly lured Cory. They met on Hastings with Dani and that girl with the birthmark, and Kayla. Until Cory, she and Kayla shared everything. She'd worn her friendship bracelet, just a grubby knotted string, until tonight. Cory used scissors to cut it off. He threw it in the garbage. Another guy had hung with them too, an older Spanish dude who tried to teach them to trill their tongues and made them laugh their heads off. He was probably dead, like Kayla and the birthmark girl.

She pressed her open palm against the window, willing him to turn around. *Let's go.* Her own reflection superimposed on his, making one person. Like her and Kayla.

Turn around. Turn around.

Maybe thoughts couldn't pass through glass.

She stepped through the sliding door. It was cold outside, but not as loud. She balanced the plate on the railing, took out her phone: 11:34. She'd give him two minutes to come over. Or text.

Before her—silver towers and golden streets, a glitter-dusted far shore. The central darkness she knew to be water. It was dotted with lights from the tankers at anchor. Earlier that night, there'd been stars, but it had clouded over, erasing the mountains.

Somebody was smoking weed. With the first skunky whiff, she felt plucked in different parts of her body. Pinched. A thousand tiny hooks piercing her skin. She checked her phone.

This time when she lifted her eyes she could tell clouds from sky. The city lit them from below. One looked like somebody floating face down in water, except her hair didn't spread but dangled like the stringy tentacles of a black jellyfish. Streaks of rain probably. How many floors up were they? The building was lifting her higher. Every darkened window in it, and in every building—blackness. Black as that beautiful moment before you open your eyes to the paramedic staring down. He's shouting your name because he knows you from before. He knows your name. You don't know his, but you recognize him by how his face glows with blue-eyed joy.

The needle is in your thigh. Then you woof.

And still Cory didn't text or see her. He was somewhere on the other side of the balcony having a great time.

She almost forgot the plate of food. She picked it up and headed back inside.

The baby was hunched on the woman's shoulder now. Small back, the little toque of T-shirt material knotted at top. Why did she think it was a boy? Had she said? No, the toque was blue.

She tried not to look at him. He was so small he made her feel like crying, which was a symptom too. Or maybe a memory. Yet there was nothing there, just the garbage bag and the things she was loading in it. Clothes. A Barbie. What did it say about you if the things you were allowed to love were packed up like trash? After so many moves, you just leave everything and go.

"Thanks," the woman said. She patted the dresser for her to set down the plate. "I'm starving."

She could grab any old purse and go now.

"Want to hold him?"

She jerked back, which made the woman laugh.

"I didn't use to like them either, believe it or not." She reached for one of the curls on the plate and let it unfurl into her mouth. Ham, it looked like. Her hand covered her chewing. "I didn't realize there'd be so many people here. Now I don't want to leave him. He's just about asleep. Then I'll go get his dad."

She just stood there, arms limp, scalp prickling, desperate now to scratch. The baby drowsed like a baby.

"I'm Miranda, by the way. Joe's sister."

"I'm Angel."

Oh, it was an angel that she'd seen from the balcony. She thought it might have been Kayla.

"That's such a pretty name. Do you have a resolution?"

She gave in, grated her scalp with her nails. "What?"

"A New Year's resolution."

"I guess. We're going away. We rented a cabin."

Cory used his mother's card. Tonight was for gas and supplies. Toilet paper and Gatorade. He'd got the list off the internet. They'd stop at the 7-Eleven on the way. Two weeks, Cory figured. New year, new life.

"Where is it?"

"What?" She hugged herself to stop from scratching.

"The cabin."

"I don't know. I don't even want to go." There were black strings hanging from the ceiling now. She swiped at one so it wouldn't touch the baby. Footsteps above.

Miranda said, "I hate travelling this time of year too. We just drove down from Penticton."

"I'm scared of trees," she said, and Miranda laughed again.

She'll put down the baby and leave sooner if you leave. Said the angel.

"Well. Bye." She backed toward the door.

"Bye," Miranda said. "Thanks!"

When she slipped into the hallway, the urge to woof came on strong. She'd seen the can earlier and now she pushed past somebody coming out, jabbed the lock. The sink was another aggravation until she got that it was magic. You had to wave your hand to turn it on. She bowed and retched. When she looked up, mascara was melting beneath her eyes. Pupils huge, leaking blackness. With her hair down she couldn't find her real self in this stranger, which made her think of the twins cross-legged on their piece of cardboard. Nobody could tell them apart so they called them Twin One and Two. Then there was only One. Or maybe Two.

And if she did go to this cabin, which was probably just some crap motel? She leaned closer to the mirror. It was already starting to leak out through her eyes—what waited for her on the other side.

Somebody touched her arm. Fat Legs from the elevator, blowing wine breath in her face and nearly sending her right back into the can.

"Jumpy!" she said, and laughed. "Michelle. I forget your name too. All I remember is Fluevog."

Michelle saw her confusion. She pointed to the green shoes, just as a tall woman in dress pants and a shiny sleeveless blouse came up and kissed her cheek.

"Miranda!" Michelle squealed.

Standing up, Miranda looked different too. "When did you get here?" Michelle asked her.

"Like, an hour ago."

"Now I remember. Angel! This is Angel."

Miranda turned to her and smiled. "I know. She saved me."

"Where's that baby?"

"Sleeping. I have to find Greg. Help me. Bye, Angel. Thanks again!"

They walked off, two chicks with jingle butts. The only thing they had to cry about.

She stopped first to switch shoes, poking a foot in the pile until she spotted an approximate 7. An actual one; it was written inside in gold. Black leather flats, black leather bows. Somebody blew a noisemaker in the other room. Bye-bye green shoes. She stuffed them in the closet.

At the bedroom door, she paused. Waves of sweat. Castanet teeth. That weird plucked-at feeling. They were coming back with Greg. She went in, grabbed the first coat in the pile that seemed her size, a puffy silver parka, cold on her arms as they entered the sleeves. The coat Cory loved was just under it. He said he loved her but if that was true, where was he?

With the elastic from her wrist she tied her hair in a top-knot. Stuck her head back out into the hall to make sure the coast was clear.

Because of the shaking, it took longer to strip the wallets and stuff her pockets. She worried too about the baby being there. Worried about him waking in a strange room.

"What do you think you're doing?"

She looked up. A man—Greg?—stood in the open door wearing glittery 2020 glasses, a basket filled with party favours hanging on one arm. One of the credit cards fell out of her pocket. She nearly heaved.

He stepped inside and, using two fingers like scissors, picked up the card and handed it to her. "Jin Hua, Official Party Animal." He lifted the glasses off. "I forbid you to leave. It's ten minutes to midnight."

It seemed then that dark hands started stirring in patterns above her. She was their marionette. She couldn't think how to get past this man and away—from the party and Cory, everything. Yet her hand tucked the credit card back into the pocket of the silver parka and closed the zipper by feel. Some tiny part of her brain was still free though, the part that knew a baby was sleeping on the other side of the room. The strings tugged her toward the door, but was the baby okay? She would worry about him all night if she didn't check, maybe for the rest of her life, which might be the same thing.

She brought her finger to her lips. The strings tightened. They wanted her to leave. Jin Hua didn't understand so she gestured for him to follow, led him around to the other side of the bed.

Together they looked down in the crib.

"Oh my God," Jin Hua gasped.

The baby was on his back, eyes closed, arms splayed out, hands in tiny fists. Was he breathing? She couldn't tell. The strings were pulling hard now, trying to drag her away. She jerked her arms to break them. Then—*duh*. She had scissors! Snip, snip, snip went her fingers, like Jin Hua had showed her.

She reached down in the crib with the flat of her hand. Warmth poured off the baby. He exhaled, or Jin Hua sighed, or she did.

"So sweet," Jin Hua said. "Whose baby is it?"

The *relief*. Strangely, it wasn't like the needle. More like the beautiful feeling pouring down on her from the paramedic's blue eyes. "Taryn? Taryn? Can you hear me? Hello, Taryn! Welcome back!" He always seemed higher than her and now she knew that he was. The dim room filled with lightness and brightness, with the tinkling of bells and her own pure wish.

Jin Hua whispered, "I think your phone's ringing."

HOW TO FAKE A BREAKDOWN

Alexandra Mae Jones

I decided that day that I was going to pretend to have a break-down because I hated my job and a mental disintegration sounded like an event that could liven it up. Years later I would have the epiphany that wanting to be insane and actually being it are functionally the same thing: No right-thinking person tries to be perceived as out of their mind and out of control. But I've been around depressed people enough to know how to mimic it. You draw into yourself like a snail hiding from rain. You stare at the inside of your skull.

When my mother lived with me, she used to take tea bags and squeeze them out over the sink for long minutes until they were dry as toast and crumbling in her hands. There was a window above our sink and she would stare out the entire time, not even looking at her hands. I imagined she was scanning for observers on the street, someone to see this odd action and marvel at it. I wanted to tell her that I was mar-velling, that I saw how unique she was, but my mother hated children more than she hated anything else. This was impres-sive because hatred was what made up her bones—she hated seemingly everything, with a cold intensity that was almost otherworldly, godlike. I idolized her.

It wasn't an old folks home where I worked: It was a "Fifty-five-plus retirement apartment complex," according to my boss, Gregory, which was a fancy way of saying an old folks home for old folks who didn't need a nurse to change their diapers yet—not like Sundown Place at the edge of town, where people got spoonfed and forgot where they were going on the way back to their rooms. No one at the apartment complex was exactly fifty-five because no one who has just turned fifty-five wants to spend all of their time with people older than fifty-five. At fifty-five, I imagine you start deliberately hanging out with thirty-year-olds and trying to psychically leech the youth out of them. Everyone at the Manor was at least seventy. I worked maintenance, despite being a hundred pounds and a woman, because it was the only job opening they had and I had connections there and not at the Tim Hortons.

"How's be?" Pat said on my way into work that day. He was washing the windows outside the main office with Xavier.

"Fair," I said. It was the same answer I gave every day.

Pat and Xavier were my co-workers. We referred to them collectively as "the boys" because they did everything together, were male, and were younger even than I was. I wasn't entirely certain they were both out of their teens. By "we," I mean Gregory and myself. Gregory was too young to live at the Manor, but old enough that I viewed him as almost a paternal figure, which was depressing considering our main interactions consisted of silent coffee breaks and him telling me about the last "young lady" who worked there.

"Dominique was a genius at this stuff. Better than any of the boys I've hired. Comes in all sorts; I don't assume nothing," he said. "She taught herself to rewire a light switch her second week she was here. I asked if her father had ever shown her how to fix things around her house or something. Didn't even have one!" He thumped his chair, thrilled. "No brothers! Single mom!"

I suspected he hoped I was going to be sauntering around the place with a tool belt and a can-do gleam in my eye within fourteen days, eager to prove Dominique was not the only woman who could learn her way around electrical innards. Of course that would've required having any form of internal drive. You don't tell your boss that you suspect your chest cavity contains a vacant, screaming hole instead of any organs, however. I smiled and asked why she didn't work here anymore. He told me chit-chat was over, and that we needed to install a new toilet in Ms. White's suite.

I'm not saying that when I worked at this place I was sad all the time, but every morning before work I did go up to the attic in my house and listen to a specific song to get some artificial energy flowing so that I could make it to work without doing something dumb like collapsing on the sidewalk.

It does not matter what song it was. Imagine the most vapid catchy pop song you know, the kind that you find yourself humming under your breath for hours until you want to chisel your eyeballs out just so you can reach into your head and yank the tune out for good. It's that song. For whatever reason I can't not dance to that song. Dancing reminds me that I have a body and that I control it.

I call it my antidepression song. It's called that as a joke. I don't really have depression. Or at least I have imposter syndrome about having depression. Is that possible? When I dropped out of university my mother said I just wanted attention. And she's probably right. I don't come by the wailing, dramatic moments honestly. I have to concoct them.

The job was not always soul-sucking. One day I demolished a wall between two suites in order to make a bigger room. When all the maintenance workers were ushered in and given the job, I expected at first that I'd be asked to stand back and let the boys handle it, but then Gregory handed me a sledgehammer. The boys didn't end up helping at all. They couldn't. As soon as the hammer was in my hands my vision narrowed down to a gunsight and I whaled on that sucker. I think Pat and Xavier knew with that singular instinct some men have about women that if anything got in my path, I would've just seen it as part of the wall—an ankle, an arm, a forehead—and would've punched through it with the weapon that felt in my hands less like a hammer than a thick, metal extension of all my anger fused into destructive purpose. It wrenched itself out of my hands at one point when I struck a beam wrong, and I gave up on it, reared back, and kicked at the panel of wood clinging to the frame until it burst through into the empty second room.

The second room had an east-facing window, and it was 9:00 a.m. Light hit my eyes, and all of existence felt suddenly, vastly open and possible before me. I had not just broadened the world; I had created it with the heel of my shoe.

In my town there was sort of an unspoken awareness that someday you'd be moving your things into the Manor. If you didn't leave soon enough, if you'd made the mistake of settling in this tiny furrow of the country, one day you'd be old and unable to make it up the stairs in your house; or your kids would want to move into the family home with their own kids because the real estate market is awful, and they'd convince you that you'd be happier living elsewhere; or you'd just be lonely and not want to eat your meals all by yourself, and so you'd end up here. Here they had bingo right after church service in the big auditorium, and a three-course meal served every lunch in a room overlooking the courtyard that I mowed diligently. The goal in this town was to die in the Manor, not at Sundown.

"I've got a parent here too," Xavier said over coffee break once. It was just the boys and me—Gregory was taking a busted-sink call. "My dad came here when Mom died and now he's got a new girlfriend. Is that like, allowed? A new girlfriend when you're pushing eighty?"

HOW TO FAKE A BREAKDOWN

"Well, how old is she?" Pat asked.

"She's also ancient. He introduced me to her the other day. I felt like I was the father and he was a teenager bringing home a prom date. Except she was sagging everywhere." He looked at me—"Sorry"—as if he'd just remembered I too was a woman, albeit in the pre-sagging stage.

"Then I think it's fine if they're the same age, right?" Pat said.

"That's not what I'm talking about," Xavier said.

How do you have a dad who is eighty when you look like you're seventeen? I wanted to ask him, but I didn't. He also looked a little like an ex of mine, which was weird because of the whole looking-seventeen thing, and the fact that the last time I saw that ex he was hightailing it out of my house with a plastic tin of pens sailing past his ear, courtesy of my mother.

Once when I was tasked with painting new yellow lines in the parking lot outside the Manor, I caught sight of Xavier through the window of an unfinished suite, nailing something to the wall inside. It was the height of summer; he had taken his shirt off. Another hand appeared in the square of the room revealed to me by the window and settled carefully on Xavier's bare back, right against that inviting curve. He went still, then tipped his head back so I could see his closed eyes, the gleam of a nail held between his teeth like an inward breath. I wanted all at once to rush the window with my can of yellow paint and splash the two of them, batter them with my stubby little paintbrush. Not because I begrudged them whatever connection they had, but because it threw my own misery into sharp relief: I on the outside of the building, painting lines that went nowhere.

These impulses itched like imagined bedbugs, all the worse for the impossibility of squashing them flat. You can't escape an idea. You can only fight it.

The day I decided to have a breakdown, I was bored.

I simply did not want to do the work I had been asked to do, and needed an excuse. Gregory had left me shut in a half-renovated suite that morning with a list of what needed to be completed before lunch. I screwed plug- and light-switch covers into the walls and put in new quarter-round, but when I got to the third task, which was to finish replacing the tiles above the toilet, I stared at the rows of chipped ceramic squares, and all the heaviness in my chest and head drained abruptly into my arms. I couldn't've lifted them if I tried.

I wanted to be found in the bathtub. There was something poetic about the image of it. A bathtub is a tiny, liminal space inside a home. A space for transition. Transformation. Naked skin enters, dirty and taxed, and emerges fresh and wrinkled with relaxation. What grown woman lies down in a bathtub at work fully clothed? It was ideal. I tipped myself into the tub without taking out the screwdrivers or the stack of fresh tiles—didn't want this to look too staged. The tub was cold and shockingly uncomfortable.

I curled around the tiles like they were a body pillow and tried to breathe evenly, staring at a pure, white spot of reflected light on the lip of the tub.

And I did a curious thing while I was lying there: At some point I left myself. I detached from my body and floated up through the apartment ceiling. I passed through walls and electrical wiring and copper plumbing pipes like they were vapour and drifted into room after room. I saw not my co-workers at work in empty suites, but the residents in their home spaces, the people who lived there who I never really thought about, and I knew them, intimately. I knew their accumulated knick-knacks and their gifts from grandchildren; I knew their loneliness and their small joys; I knew the way boredom nestled like a cold, dead thing around the breastbone. I knew they loved and hated each other in private dramas that did not include me.

I watched Emily Nguyen move her mouth into wide shapes in front of the mirror, pretending with a hand on her ribbed throat that she could still belt out songs if she just mimicked the look of it. I watched three women on the second floor gossip in the laundry room about how Patricia Lee had left her tummy-trainer spandex balled up in a dryer, and I knew they were really saying to each other, *I hate you, I hate me, I hate this.* I watched Pierre Desportes carefully wrapping up his wife's jewellery piece by piece in tissue paper for his daughter to take with her when she visited later to bring him to the funeral home. I watched Mary of room 201B apply clothespins, upright and painful, across Esther Jacob's bare stomach, pinching skin into a peak, in Esther's sitting room where they met to talk about their late husbands every week, and I knew that this action had started as a joke about the way their skin hung loose on their skeletons now, but had turned into something almost erotic and meaningful, something they had waited for for years—laughter choked down into this quiet moment of Esther clutching at Mary's shoulder and pretending the nipping of pulled skin was why she was tearing up.

Shelly was five days from death, and that's how she could see me. It was the culmination of her affair with Howard and he had fallen asleep before she was done, with his penis still inside her, the two of them spooned on his bed. She tried to laugh, but instead found herself punching the covers again and again, wishing she'd picked a different man, a different life, wishing her son hadn't dumped her in this place, feeling her heart batter itself inside her throat, on its last legs. "This is none of your business," she hissed when she saw me floating above them. She swiped a hand up, and when I reached for it, her palm passed through mine, so cold.

There was only one room I couldn't see into. When I hovered past it, it bled black at me like an inked out censor.

After a while I became bored of this, too, and returned to the tub.

The light in the room had changed, shrinking across the floor. It was colder now, the morning long past.

I realized that no one was going to walk into the apartment I'd been tasked with renovating. None of my co-workers would stumble upon me, curled in the bathtub in this dramatic, tragically romantic fashion, with my hands cradled just so, and feel a sudden swell of mortal fear for my physical and mental well-being. The fact of it was that no one thought about me enough to go looking for me after I didn't show up for lunch. A retirement home is one where you go to disappear. I had achieved this much earlier in life than I was supposed to.

I climbed out of the bathtub with difficulty, and set about roaming the halls of the Manor until someone saw me. Porcelain dust in my hair, a screwdriver dangling from my hand. Tiny, shuffling steps. I fixed my gaze somewhere in the middle distance and adopted an expression of exquisite woe.

Gregory came upon me first. Before I could even stutter out my carefully framed story, he looked me head to toe and said, "You don't look too good, you can take off early."

Take off early? That was it?

I tottered to the break room to get my things. On my way out my feet led me to the door that I had been unable to see behind when I was floating. The blacked-out room. It wasn't locked, so I went in, still moving in that halting, rocking way in case Gregory saw me and realized I was faking all of this instability.

I'd always known which room was hers because I helped her move in, but I'd been in here so rarely that it was still somehow a surprise when I realized who I was looking at. The original. The mould into which I had poured myself. She was in a leather recliner, watching the Shopping Channel with her eyes half-closed.

'It's me,' I said.

My mother shifted her hand—a flick as though a fly had landed on her.

"My shift isn't up yet, but I fell asleep in a bathtub," I said. "Gregory said I could go home early."

There must have been, somewhere inside her head, a tiny room where she had boxed away all her care for me. There was no way she could truly feel nothing for a thing that she put so much work into. I tore her open on my way out. That's not a nothing feeling. If I could just bring my sledgehammer inside her maybe I could do that again, knock down the walls that keep her emotions segmented and find that room dedicated to me.

"A bathtub," I repeated. "But I'm fine."

She turned her head, as slow and even as an android. Her eyes were so pale her pupils looked hole-punched into her skull. She said nothing, but I was fluent in her expressions. I thought about smashing her TV, but I would just have to fix it or install a new one the next day. I thought next about Shelly, how I knew that her heart would pop soon in her sleep, how relaxing it would be to close your eyes and just have that be it.

I've decided I will tell you the song after all. My antidepression song. The name doesn't matter, just that it's the Jessie J song that no one remembers is Jessie J because it sounds like a knock-off Katy Perry song. There's a line in the chorus that talks about 'dirty dancing in the moonlight.' And I know that's meant to be grinding, that awful, jerking upright-humping thing men with no rhythm do against women's asses, but I always hear it as *Dirty Dancing*. Like watching that movie under the stars.

And I'm in a flowing pink dress, out under this glowing moon on a wide, rolling hill of grass, with trees and a pond to reflect the moon and make it twice as bright, and it's dark out, sure, it's night, but it's all an inky blue instead of black and somehow my dress is lit so brightly you can still see that it's pink. And I run and leap into the air with full confidence, and I'm caught, I'm lifted up by strong, certain hands, hands that love me, hands that will catch me every time I do this. And I can't die, really—see, it's an antidepression song—because I have to reach that moment with the dress and the hands and the soaring, caught, captured, held, weightless feeling of freedom and safety all at the same time.

PALAIS ROYALE

Tamas Dobozy

The Chip-Chip Duo always looked like they were playing a funeral, unless they were playing a funeral, in which case they looked just right. Lyle Jakes had seen it—he'd been stalking them for months, sitting through performances in Hungarian restaurants and bars, at cultural events, weddings, baptisms, funeral receptions. The two men looked so much alike they might have been twins. Ferenc played a saxophone, Miklós played a synthesizer, standing behind a big square of cardboard with the words *Chip-Chip Duo* written on it in golden glitter. Everyone knew who they were—the Csíp brothers—but they insisted on the sign, as if there was some chance of mistaking them for the Miles Davis Quintet. Jakes's image of them was locked into step-up stages, the red-velvet-and-folk-motif decor of restaurants at one-fifth capacity, two or three older couples dancing listlessly on the linoleum to some ancient favourite to make Ferenc and Miklós feel better, playing debutante balls with few or no debutantes. Not that the Chip-Chip Duo ever complained, or displayed emotion. Whether playing for a hundred people or playing for none, their faces were as neutral as steel. When the basket went around Jakes rubbed his eyes and stared into it a long time before catching the glint of coins nestled in a five, and he wondered if that was all they got paid, and if that was why both of them had to take music students on the side.

Those boys really needed a manager.

Jakes was a third as old as the Chip-Chip Duo and had recently finished a BBA at the Morgenstern School of Business, failing to demonstrate either the grades or the talent necessary to get into the co-op program. He'd graduated summa cum mediocris, not a stitch of work experience or outstandingness to his name, except for an unholy perseverance. He knew there were thousands like him out there, lost tribes of the corporate corridor, clutching their diplomas like mayday flags. But one thing he could be sure of: he was the only one who could see—after a lifetime of experience—the future in failure. He was, at the risk of sounding self-important, a connoisseur of shit.

And that winter was for sure the season of shit. It was the winter Hesse's Emporium opened an "outsider art" LP section, crowds of hipsters scouring the bins for rare finds—country and western albums recorded by middle-aged men with names like George, Guido, and Tony on four tracks in the basement; the entire series of recordings, made and sold surreptitiously, of Heato Valve and the Hottones, who'd played Perry Como covers for quarters at College and Spadina between 1977 and 1979; the skinhead band the Adolph Sitler Section and their awful covers of Motown and klezmer hits. It was the winter Jakes watched people flock to consignment stores along Queen West and East for the latest in '70s kitsch—corduroy couches, tasselled lampshades, velvet painting of dogs playing poker. It was the winter of Horst Wasser's collages made from cut-up war-amp calendars selling for thousands in commercial galleries.

Jakes had a theory. Irony did play a role in all of it, but a minor one. Those who were attracted to this crap laughed only so long. After that, your appreciation crossed into another,

more earnest zone—the sadness of artworks laboured on
across a lifetime, marked by an ambition ending in failure,
abjection, tears. This was bad art made by *real* people, not the
great talents, the visionaries, the geniuses, but the rest of us,
and they spoke more directly, more intimately, of that tragedy—of everyday humanity—than any masterpiece. That
winter everyone was tired of the irrelevance of aesthetics,
high style, good taste.

Not one course in the BBA had prepared Jakes for this.
No doubt, the instructors would have said there was a con-
tradiction in the idea of managing bad art. But logical con-
tradiction, Jakes knew, was only an impediment in the mind,
not in the world. Real life might be nothing but logical con-
tradiction. Didn't they know there was plenty of good stuff
among the old art filling up museums the world over? Another
masterpiece! How many masterpieces did the human race
need? Besides, if you could manage the Ice Capades or professional wrestling or hot-dog eating contests, why not the
Chip-Chip Duo? The problem—he realized, sitting in front
of Miklós and Ferenc playing the theme to *The Dukes of
Hazzard*—was that the BBA people had no imagination.
They were looking for coal seams of quality when they were
in a diamond mine of shit. Surrounded by the stuff! It was an
insight you had to have suffered for, Jakes knew it better than
anyone.

But what kept him up at night—and Jakes was often up
at night, sleeping in hour snatches, waking to his heart like
a jackhammer, brain whirring with plans—wasn't what
his instructors thought, but the fact that originality didn't
exist. If he had realized the market in bad art, no doubt some
other BBA grad had realized it too, and was even now eyeing
the Chip-Chip Duo and the other hot acts. That's why Jakes
needed to sign them first—all of them. He settled deeper into
his chair, so sleep deprived there were figures in the corners of
his vision. Bursts of colour—blue and white. He was so tired

there wasn't a tune he couldn't sit in front of. Nothing made it through. His fatigue as thick and protective as lead.

The Chip-Chip Duo played instrumental covers of everything: theme songs from TV shows; Beatles, Led Zeppelin, Sex Pistols hits; old *sláger* melodies; dumbed-down "best of's" from Mozart, Brahms, Beethoven; improvisations on anything you could hum. Ferenc's saxophone was plastic. Miklós's canned beats and notes sounded as if they were plastic too. You'd swear they made the music bad on purpose, though if you talked to them, say between sets at the Duna Vendéglő on the first Saturday of every month, they would have told you in no uncertain terms that they were artists. I am a musician first, Miklós said, playing a quick chord progression. This is a premier venue. The acoustics in this place really bring out our microtones. Not a flicker of a smile to his face. You keep coming up here to ask us, but the answer is the same: Why would we need a manager when everything is going so well? We— he motioned to his brother, who nodded—we have achieved *everything* we ever dreamed of. It has taken us many, many years.

They were serious men, professorial, spouting music theory as if they'd invented it and then slouching back to the bandstand to play a waltzified "Back in Black" with an indifference so cool, so studied, that many of the younger people in the audience—there for the exquisite badness of the music— nearly fell off their chairs laughing. Jakes scowled, less because they were laughing (entertainment was entertainment after all), but because listening closely, for the first time ever, he heard something underneath it: stray notes scattered like marbles across a warped floor. He wondered: maybe it was just something a good night of sleep could cure.

On the walk home from the Duna Vendéglő that night, Jakes decided on a new tactic: He'd apply to take piano lessons from Miklós. Maybe if he showed enthusiasm for music they'd know he was serious about managing them.

He showed up for his first lesson two weeks later. The apartment was austere as a biomedical facility. Most of it was taken up with industrial shelves piled high with scores, LPs, cassette tapes, CDs, VHS, Betamax, even laser discs—every available technology recent or obsolete. The music was, without exception, by composers Jakes didn't recognize, never mind associate with the Chip-Chip Duo—Schoenberg, Stravinsky, Bartók—segueing into ever more unlistenable stuff—Boulez, Feldman, Babbitt, Stockhausen, Ligeti, Kurtág, Murail, Cendo. Music too remote for most people to stay in the same room with, not to mention pay for. The afternoon sun sat on it like glaze, and Jakes was sweating by the time they sat at the piano, a baby grand, which took up most of the floor space in the tiny apartment. How had Miklós gotten it inside? By crane? There was a framed picture on the lid, a portrait of Miklós and Ferenc and someone else, all young, all clearly related, maybe even triplets, wearing tuxedos on an art deco stage, the arches and pillars covered in glittering leaves.

Who's that guy there? Jakes asked. Another brother? Miklós looked at him like he'd gone blind, or night had fallen and he was searching for the source of a strange voice. Was there once a Chip-Chip-Chip Trio? Miklós looked at him as if he was the purest of idiots, distilled to imbecility. That, he finally said, is me. Jakes waited a minute, looking back at the photograph. No, he protested, I mean the other guy. That is Ferenc, Miklós replied. The third guy! Miklós was silent, and for a second Jakes thought he wasn't going to answer. That is not a guy, he finally said. *That* is a woman. Jakes peered at the photograph as if his eyes could tear away the phony moustache, or pierce the shirt like X-rays. A woman? Miklós nodded, gazing around as if the room was enveloped in darkness. C'mon, Jakes said, that's totally a dude! Okay, shrugged Miklós, with the same indifference he showed onstage, and which Jakes imagined he would have shown anywhere, during an earthquake, say, or some mass extinction event such as a comet crashing into the

41

earth. Okay, it's a *dude*. Jakes waited for him to elaborate, but Miklós did not.

Flustered, Jakes said, Have you ever thought of getting a manager? No, the old man replied, only of killing one. Is that why you are here? Why you are taking lessons? You must give up this idea. Nothing good can come of it. Believe me.

Jakes would ponder this for a week, tossing and turning on the sheets. How could not having a manager be a good thing?

He was still thinking about it on the night of Nate Inkster's watercolor exhibit. The show was scheduled at Painterly Place, a gallery aspiring artists could rent to exhibit their works. Or at least that had been the original intent, but it had ended up attracting failed artists more than aspiring ones. Ten, fifteen, twenty years failed, though still filled with hope, still giving it their all. That winter, it was this earnestness that turned the place—empty most nights except for the artists themselves, or an occasional friend come out of duty, or someone who'd wandered in for the free wine and peanuts—into a celebration of disgrace. "Transcendent ineptitude," was how one critic put it. Painterly Place was suddenly hot with the hipster crowd. The owner, wanting to capitalize, started charging an entry fee, first a dollar, then two, sums so slight, so much worse than asking for nothing at all, they further eroded what credibility the exhibits might have had, and word spread further. Now it was the place to be whenever there was an opening. You went down a set of iron stairs from street level into a room too tight with bodies, overheated, all of them pointing with excitement and laughing. Jakes had been waiting for the right moment to sign Inkster, waiting for him to hit rock bottom in other words, when he'd seek out Jakes's protection from that terrible laughter breaking on him wave after wave, like the sea in those naval disasters that were his sole subject matter. He'd only received one critical notice, during the 2014 ArtWalk in Toronto. *NOW* magazine had written: "You'll see everything from works-in-progress by impressive up-and-comers such as Lillian Trockl to painstakingly bad imitations of real art, as in the watercolours of Nate Inkster."

That night, Inkster stood crestfallen in a corner, stammering when someone approached to shake his hand and ask how in the heck did he manage to paint like that. Inkster would adjust his glasses and pull his sweat-soaked shirt from his chest and say, Well, I'm just starting out. By the end of the night, every painting had sold, at exceedingly low prices. Most would end up in basement toilets or fraternity game rooms or as prank housewarming gifts for couples who'd wonder how soon was too soon to throw them out. Inkster was preternaturally gifted at being terrible—maybe even a genius at it—but he needed an attitude adjustment. Showing his stuff here made it look as if his terribleness was involuntary, as if he was trying for something better, which of course he was, though that was hardly the point. If the paintings had shown at a commercial gallery it would have looked as if he'd done it by design, and patrons would have paid top dollar.

Before the doors closed, Jakes hid in a bathroom stall, comfortable in the heat, his eyelids falling lower and lower. When he awoke, to the long squeal of a door, Inkster was in front of the mirror, trying to pat down a few hairs where his skull peaked in a kind of ridge. Jakes exited the stall, breathing heavily. You again! Inkster turned. He was snarling, but there was a sob deep beneath it. Listen, Inkster, all I want is for you to embrace your greatness. Oh God, Inkster said. He held a hand across his brow against the harsh fluorescence shining behind Jakes. Just give me a chance, Jakes said. Did you see it out there? Inkster replied. They were laughing. Well, your stuff is very good, Jakes said. Inkster looked like he was going to attack, but in the end he withered. You could smell the sweat on him like vinegar from an old watchband. There's no place for tragedy in art anymore, Jakes continued. Comedy is the new tragedy. The universe is ludicrous. That's what you've latched on to: men leaping from torpedoed ships; drowning in fiery oil slicks; torn apart by sharks. All done in that luminous paint-by-numbers style of yours. But Inkster shook his head in disagreement. The universe, he muttered, is a place of profound mystery. It reveals its perfection even in the most savage of moments. Jakes gaped at him. My God, he finally said, that's perfect. You've got to let me represent you. Inkster scowled so hard he trembled, and turned away from Jakes.

He was close to breaking, Jakes could sense it. If only the man could find the strength to commit, to realize how good he could be by being bad, without becoming self-conscious when he sat down to paint and trying to be that way on purpose. Listen, he said. I've been where you're at. Rock bottom. It was the third year of my BBA. No matter how hard I studied, how much I sucked up to the profs, I just couldn't figure it out. My roommates were making the dean's list, networking, lining up jobs, scoring chicks. Whenever I asked how they did it they just laughed and told me I didn't have a chance. I know, looking at me now, it's hard to believe! I'm not going to lie to you, Inkster. One night I sat down with a bottle of Tylenol 3s, jumbo size, and a twenty-sixer of Southern Comfort. Started shooting the pills, one after another. Then five at a time. About a half hour into it my roommates came in. They were supposed to have been gone for the weekend. Some big party in the Muskokas. Forgot their condoms or weed or something. They looked at me and you know what they said? *Tylenol.* One word, that's it. Then they burst out laughing. And you know what I said? I'm glad I'm so entertaining for you. They laughed their heads off. You're not much, Jakes, they said, but when it comes to being pathetic, you're fucking king! That was it, Jakes said, bringing his face so close to Inkster's the old man could feel the eyeballs graze his skin. The moment. Shit can have its victory, too. Jakes kept his face there, like a beacon. They pissed all over me. You know that? What you experienced out there—it's nothing, ignore it. But for me it was a shower of gold. The old man took a step back, but it only made Jakes lean in farther. You could be a king, too. Come on, he shouted, slapping Inkster on the shoulder. Sell their derision back to them! Don't you get it? Let's meet tomorrow and sign a contract. He thrust a business card at him like a knife. The old man reached for it, tentatively. Fuckin' crazy, he muttered, and Jakes nodded. That's why it'll work. He was sure now that he had Inkster on the hook. His first client. They'd book another slot, a month from now, at the Painterly. They'd double the cover charge to four dollars. Inkster could give a lecture: "The Mysteries of the Universe." They'd invite important people. It would be like stand-up, with the audience laughing at everything except the punch line.

Before leaving the gallery, Jakes looked back. Inkster stood like a bent nail in the light of the bathroom door, so harsh it rendered everything in black and white. The old man's head and shoulders glowed as if he had a halo, but it was continually being sucked away by the darkness of the gallery. Inkster was peering closely at the gold lettering on the business card, and Jakes couldn't help but feel it was a promising sign, as if the artist was finally giving his offer the consideration it deserved.

He leaped up the stairs into the night. Signing Inkster would make it easier to sign the Chip-Chip Duo. He could see the future: a flash office in a mall off Steeles, the words *So Bad It's Good Management Incorporated* in flashing lights above the entryway. With a dozen acts like the Chip-Chip Duo and Inkster, he could put on an arts festival. That night, Jakes couldn't sleep for dreaming, one fevered fantasy after another, and in the morning he drank an entire pot of coffee, determined to take another run at Miklós.

He turned up early for piano lessons. Today was the day he signed the Chip-Chip Duo! Jakes lifted a hand to knock on the battered tin door but then paused. What the fuck was that? He pressed his ear to the cladding. There was no melody he could make out, only a scattering of notes, as if leaking from holes in the score, dribbling away, none of them happy in each other's company. It took Jakes several minutes to realize it was the sound he'd heard weeks ago, intricate and sinister, beneath the Chip-Chip Duo's cover tunes. Miklós seemed lost in the playing, as if unaware of what time it was, but when the clock hit fifteen minutes past the hour he stopped and the door was wrenched open and there stood Jakes, bent to one side, hand cupped around an ear. Are you eavesdropping on me? Jakes froze, unsure of how listening to music could be classified as eavesdropping. The woman in the picture was my sister, Miklós hissed. Her name was Louise. Greatest composer I've ever played. He put a finger to his lips and glared for a minute at Jakes, who didn't dare say a word, still crouched there in awe of the man's fury. There was something beautiful in it, burning red and orange in the midst of the tin and grey of the apartment corridor, like the discovery of antique wallpaper under a coat of paint. No more piano lessons for you, hissed Miklós. He slammed the door.

Jakes fled in a daze. Was it supposed to be this hard? Didn't Miklós want to make money at the same time as he made art? Did one have to preclude the other? And who was Louise? Was she the secret behind Miklós's art? Or was she a riddle, a challenge posed to him, what Jakes needed to sort out in order to finally sign the Chip-Chip Duo?

He went to the Toronto Public Library. Jakes hadn't been to one in a long time, way before his BBA days, probably when he was still in elementary school. In university he'd only gotten as far as the front doors of the library, where he'd met a guy on two separate occasions, both times to buy a term paper. He didn't have the money for an A, so he'd settled for the B- version, the minimum mark needed to stay in the program. Jakes had tried to fix up the first paper a bit, hoping for a better grade, but had gotten a C+, and had to petition to stay in the program. The next paper he left alone and it squeaked through. The guy he'd bought them from had won the Graduate Dean's Achievement Award for the highest GPA in the program. He could nail any grade he wanted, and after that Jakes felt as if he'd learned something important from him on the virtues of precision, being open to opportunities, making sure you had several irons in the fire, etc.

Now he wandered the stacks. A librarian took pity on Jakes and led him to a reference desk. Are you looking for something in particular, Mr. . . ? Lyle, he replied. Lyle Jakes. He looked around conspiratorially, then spoke without meeting the woman's gaze, as if her brains were in her lap. I'm looking for information you might have on a woman named Louise Csíp. Well, then, let's see what we have, the librarian said, in a way that was so professionally friendly, so totally directed at no one in particular, that it could only be aggression. Down deep she hated him, Jakes knew it.

They spent the afternoon chasing traces. The deeper they went the more driven the librarian seemed, pausing at nothing, including whole pages of Hungarian that came up on computer or microfiche. They scanned so much print it felt to Jakes as if the jagged letters were miles of barbed wire intended to keep him from Miklós and Ferenc. There was a fair bit on someone called Lajos Csíp, of the famed Csíp Piano Trio from the 1920s and '30s. Ferenc and Miklós would have been young then, in their late teens or early twenties. Lajos had studied under Bartók during the 1910s, and been friendly with Kodály. He'd produced ten, maybe eleven, pieces (the scholars were divided on attribution), all held in high regard, though more for their promise than for what they did. The trio left the country in the mid-1930s, terrified of Horthy and fascism. For a few years they performed in North America, mainly in New York, Chicago, Boston, Montreal, and Toronto, the city in which they finally settled. The critical notices were not great. In fact, each one seemed worse than the last. One of them said Lajos played "as if his arms were made of concrete, his fingers of iron." The last performance, in late 1938, at the Palais Royale in Toronto, was a disaster, with the crowd walking out, and Lajos being carried from the stage. The trio disappeared after that. The librarian found no other information on them. Not even an obituary. Maybe they're all still alive, Jakes said.

The librarian frowned, her fore and middle fingers lightly tapping the *J* and *K* keys, back and forth. What about the Heißes Blechbläserquartett? she asked. What Heißes Blechbläserquartett? Jakes replied. She swiveled the screen toward him. It was a grainy poster from prewar Germany: four men, though the fourth could have been a woman, his hair was so long. Favourites in Weimar, from the looks of it, the librarian said. Dance band. Played so-called *Negermusik*, which the Nazis would later ban, though Hitler secretly loved it, What's the connection? Jake said. The librarian shook her head as if Jakes's question was so many flies buzzing in her face, and pointed to the caption: "*Das Heiße Blechbläserquartett: Alois, Franz, Micha, Jockel Csíp, März 22, 1936.*" She hit another tab on her browser and up came an old *Toronto Star* article. They read it together. One of the band members, Jockel, was picked up in 1939 and sent to Auschwitz. The other three made it out before the start of the war. Alois, Franz, Micha. They ended up enlisting, playing in the Royal Canadian Artillery Band. Afterwards, they played in and around Toronto, Ottawa, Montreal, places south. Look, they played the Palais Royale, too, the librarian said. The show got terrible reviews, though. She brought up a sidebar from 1952, reviewing a number of live acts from the night before. It reported that Micha and Alois both had black eyes onstage. The music sounded like they were attacking each other with notes, hurling them back and forth, while Franz adjusted his horn second by second, trying to play referee, to recover the melody. A punch-drunk performance if ever there was one. "It appears the Csíp brothers are no longer content to keep their fisticuffs backstage," the reviewer reported.

Jakes had no time to digest this before the librarian asked, What about the Chip Chamber Orchestra? What? Jakes was flabbergasted. How many members? Five. Louis, Francis, Michael, Jacob, George. Their last name was Chip? The librarian rolled her eyes. They also played the Palais Royale, she said, going straight to the emerging pattern. Not legally, though. The librarian flicked lint off her suit jacket whenever Jakes looked at her. It was during the so-called Impresario Action, the weekend of June 24–26, 1949. Concerted protests by musicians in Toronto against hiring practices in certain venues. A bunch of break-ins and impromptu takeovers of the stage. She pointed to an article and Jakes scanned it, amazed at how much information was available to people who did research. The Chip brothers, referred to in the article as second-generation Hungarian, had managed to play several pieces—Dvořák, Bartók, Debussy—before police battered their way through the crowd to the stage. The bandleader, Michael, made a statement to the press afterwards, accepting full responsibility for the orchestra's part in the protest. He was in tears. During the melee, his brother Louis's left hand was smashed with a baton, resulting in severe nerve damage. The Chip Chamber Orchestra would never play again.

Jakes could feel sweat break out at the roots of his hair, and when the librarian looked at him sideways, like she'd done all she could, like he was dismissed, he lost it. There was supposed to be very little information, he yelled. Almost none! Now there's probably a Csíp sextet, septet, or … a frickin' Csíp philharmonic! He stomped his foot. What am I supposed to do with all this? The librarian raised an eyebrow. You think you'd be happy. You know how many people I get in here looking for something they can't find? They'd love to be in your position. Nobody would love to be in my position, snarled Jakes. Well, you're probably right about that, muttered the librarian. Jakes stomped out. The research was endless. Disappointed old men from here to the horizon!

Now it was Ferenc's turn to be approached, Jakes decided. The problem was, Ferenc seemed even more aloof than Miklós. When Jakes visited his apartment to ask about saxophone lessons, the old man shrugged. That was it: a shrug. Jakes shook his head, then started to speak, So, that means. . . ? Ferenc shrugged again and slammed the door in his face. Jakes wondered if Miklós had warned Ferenc about him ahead of time.

He would have to follow Ferenc everywhere, even if it meant around-the-clock surveillance. He would not sleep until he'd broken through. He would watch for habits, patterns of behavior, that would expose his vulnerabilities. That's how you successfully exploited people—by zeroing in on their weaknesses. The BBA had taught him that. For instance, Inkster's Achilles heel was confidence, he needed someone to instill it. But the Chip-Chip Duo were something else. They were too self-sufficient, secretive. There were no cracks.

The first day Ferenc went to a laundromat and grocery store. Jakes hid in the street to keep an eye on him, and ended up catching a cold, rising the next morning in a delirium of sleeplessness and fever. That day Ferenc visited a clothing store and a Tim Hortons, buying a double-double plus a jelly doughnut, and after that sat for awhile in a park. Then he went home. Jakes returned to his apartment and drew up a list of things they might talk about: laundry, groceries, clothing, bad coffee, fat pastries, and public parks. It would not, he decided, be a very illuminating conversation. The next day was the coldest so far in February, minus thirty with wind-chill, and Ferenc was bundled against it in an overcoat to his ankles, a toque, and a scarf wound so high around his neck he looked like a spool of yarn. He strolled down Roncesvalles to Budapest Park by the lakeshore, lingered a moment by the monument to the fallen of 1956, hands crossed, lips moving in prayer. Then Ferenc strolled toward a squat art deco building a little farther east. The Palais Royale had once been a ballroom, but was now locked up, lost in years of legal wrangling between the city and developers.

The old man lingered in front of the façade. Basie and Ellington had played here. The house band had been fronted by Lyle Niosi, Canada's "King of Swing," long forgotten. Probably didn't have a good manager.

Ferenc walked to the side of the building and began testing windows. He was not nimble for a man of his age and when he finally found an open one it took forever to climb inside, with a great popping of buttons, untucking of shirt, snagging of pants, wrenching of elbows and knees, and an epic of swearing. Jakes waited, then followed, climbing inside with equal difficulty. He heard the click of Ferenc's heels up ahead, beyond the frosted lamps, the framed photographs across the years, the mid-1950s minimalism of sofas and chairs. Peeking around a corner, he saw Ferenc onstage, nodding at ghosts who'd once come to dance the Charleston, the jitterbug, the foxtrot. He stood without moving, hands to either side, as if shushing an audience. He was king here, in a kingdom of silence. He stood there so long Jakes's right leg started to cramp, and his neck too, from holding himself in position. It felt like a hot wire snaking through his sciatic nerve. He needed to shift, but doing so would have required him to be more silent than the silence of the Palais Royale. Was this how the audience had felt the night of those performances by the various Csíp bands?

Unable to ignore the pain any longer, Jakes shifted behind the corner, then peeked out again. But Ferenc was gone. The stage was empty. Jakes looked around, then stepped out. He couldn't feel his leg, and he almost fell, barely managing to get a foot out in front of himself. The ballroom wavered with the cold light of waves reflected from the lake. Jakes went up onstage cautiously, looked around, parted the curtain. He could hear footsteps far off, down the corridor to the dressing rooms, and now Jakes moved quick, still on tiptoe, like some fiend driven past the old sandbags and props and ropes on pulleys, down the dusty hall to dressing room 4. The old man was sitting on a chair, staring into a mirror ringed by bulbs, though only three of them still burned, flickering with an electrical crackle then dying out again. He lifted earbuds to either ear, swirling his thumb across a tiny screen. Oh God, Jakes thought, this is it, the answer to everything. The old man was taunting him. What should he do? Reveal himself or stay hidden? Slowly, the old man started tapping his feet. The beat was off-kilter. It was no beat at all. You couldn't move to it, backward or forward. It was a wall. The old man started singing. It sounded like a moan pouring from an oil drum. Now he was trilling like a bird. The bulbs flickered and Jakes drew back. It wasn't Ferenc. Or was it? He waited for the bulbs to flicker again, and he was sure of it. The resemblance was close—the same narrow forehead, ridged nose, knife-thin lips—but that wasn't the face he'd followed into this place. It was like Ferenc had made microscopic adjustments to himself, barely noticeable in the bits and pieces, but adding up to something else entirely. Jakes turned quietly before the old man caught a glimpse of him in the mirror, and fled still on tiptoe up the stairs, across the backstage, out onto the bandstand, where he just caught the tail end of another figure disappearing down a corridor.

That must be Ferenc, he thought, slowing, taking short quick steps. He peered down the corridor and saw a door close near the end. Fuck, he thought, glancing back at the stage, expecting any minute to see the curtain part on that old man from the dressing room. He crept quickly along the wall, ready to flatten himself if necessary. The door at the end was for the men's room. Maybe it'll be okay if I just go in, Jakes thought. Maybe he'll think I'm just another one of the . . . One of the what? Who was that old man in the dressing room? Sweating around the eyes, Jakes pulled the door open a crack. The bathroom was overwarm, dry, lit by a wall of translucent glass that cast a dead light over everything. The old man had his back to Jakes. He was practicing a dance move, the same one, over and over, muttering something under his breath that sounded like the cracking of walnuts. His elbows were up, his feet sandpapering the floor. When he turned slightly Jakes realized it wasn't Ferenc. Same forehead, nose, lips, but nothing else. The eyes had seen a different story.

Jakes closed the door and leaned against the wall, its plaster cooling the sweat running down his back. At the opposite end of the corridor a figure opened a door, glared at him a minute, then closed it. Aha, thought Jakes. But he felt exposed in the radiance of the exit sign, as if it was ultraviolet, illuminating the fear on his skin. The door opened on a concrete stairwell, down into an underground parking garage. Jakes paused in front of a wall of safety glass. Somewhere down there a car horn was bleeting a series of arpeggios. It wasn't four-four time exactly. The last beat was a fraction. Three and three-fifths? Jakes took a deep breath and went through. Inside, the reverberations of the horn hit with such force it felt like his teeth were being chipped away. Jakes tried not to smile but it was always how terror played him. He'd smile, thinking it would help if he showed how badly he wanted to be liked. Abruptly, the horn was joined by another. Jakes turned in the direction of a car door slamming. There was an old man behind the wheel. It had to be Ferenc. But it wasn't. So close—but it wasn't him. The ferocity in the eyes was different somehow, less cultivated, crazy, wild. He turned on his headlights and Jakes shielded his eyes. Half a second later there was another slam, from farther down. This, too, was a rhythm, Jakes realized. He saw another old man get into a car as another horn joined in. His face was like a map of Ferenc's face, not the same, but meant to lead him to it. Another door slammed somewhere else. Another horn started up. Amazing how organized it still sounded, the din of it, ear-splitting crescendos, as if there was an intelligence, a compositional skill, beneath the cacophony. A third headlight came on, a fourth. Engines started up, and Jakes was running, running and running, up the steps, down the corridor, back to the open window he'd first entered, finding it even more difficult to get through, his body bent into various angles—the crook of knees, hinge of elbows, his chin buried in his chest so the top of his head could clear the frame—pushing his body through in a scraping of skin, twisting of ligaments, bending of bone.

He ran into the parking lot and kept running until he'd crossed up and over the Roncesvalles Pedestrian Bridge, collapsing on a public bench at the corner of Queen. Jakes hadn't felt this way since the night his roommates stood over him laughing as he retched Tylenol into the toilet. He'd never told anyone the full story, not even Inkster, who probably could have used it, thought Jakes, looking back at the Palais Royale. The wind whipped the hair back and forth in front of his eyes like windshield wipers. His body was shaking with a feeling somewhere between panic and ecstasy.

Jakes took out his list of conversation topics for Ferenc and crossed off the Palais Royale so forcefully the pen tore the paper. He'd heard of artists testing their potential managers, but this was beyond anything.

He pulled out his phone, nearly in tears, and dialed Miklós, demanding to know what had just happened, but panicked the minute it started ringing and quickly hung up. If he started talking now, crazed as he was, Miklós would ask him what he thought he'd seen, how long it had been since he slept, were there even now motes of light dancing in his eyes? Jakes tried to brush them out of the air, but they seemed to slip through his fingers like brightly coloured beads, and he realized he had no good answer for Miklós, not yet. He stared at the receiver, thinking he had to assert himself somehow, then dialed a different number. It rang forever—seven, eight, nine times— before a hollow voice came on: Nate Inkster is not at home, might not be for awhile actually, but if you have any interest in speaking at him, a little or at length, even if you just want to tell him something to get it over with so you won't have to talk to him anymore, really anything is welcome, even an insult, then leave a message after the beep. Jakes waited a second, amazed at the man, then said: Inkster! You better be preparing new work for our show. Jakes remembered what he'd read online; it came babbling out of his mouth. Listen, he said, you ever hear about the *Wilhelm Gustloff*? German troop trans- port. Sunk in 1945 by a Soviet submarine. We're talking Baltic Sea, temperatures well below freezing. Three torpedoes. Most died instantly, the rest from exposure, or were trampled in the panic to get to the lifeboats. Ten thousand in all. Paint it up!

Jakes strolled quickly home, packed ice into a bag, put it on top of his head, feeling it cool his brain. Did the Chip- Chip Duo really have the kind of resources they'd just put on display at the Palais Royale? How many old men were there? Jakes had to admit it: this changed things. It was an exponen- tial leap. There was no limit to the kinds of shows they could do now. The Chip-Chip-Chip Trio, the Chip-Chip-Chip-Chip Quartet, the Chip-Chip-Chip-Chip-Chip Quintet, and so on. Jakes pressed the ice into his scalp. He hadn't thought about anything this hard ever. Such concentration sure would have been useful during the BBA. At 3:00 a.m. he fell asleep still fully clothed, in a fit of sweat, tossing back and forth on the couch.

In the dream, he called Miklós. Your brother was effemin- ate. You mocked and bullied him, called him Louisa, though you recognized his talent. You forced him to take you and Fer- enc in the trio, though your abilities were mediocre at best. You forced him to leave Hungary because you thought there'd be more money out here. To get even, he started playing badly. Worse and worse until you guys were ruined. Every couple of weeks you'd smack the shit out of him, but that only strength- ened his resolve. Then, one night, backstage at the Palais Royale, you hit him too hard, and you and Ferenc have been punishing yourselves ever since.

Can't hear a thing you're saying, replied Miklós, hanging up.

In the dream, Jakes dialed again. Your brother Lajos wanted to be a woman. But he couldn't be. The times were not right. He played music like an angel. Poured his repressed soul into it. But as the years went by, as the war dragged on, after you came out here, it started killing him, day by day, until finally he couldn't play at all. The sorrow of the tragedy murdered your and Ferenc's ambition, your talent. That's when you started playing schmaltz.

Hello? Hello? said Miklós. Anyone there? He hung up.

Jakes dialed again. You're dreaming, he said. Stop this. But his dream-self refused. Lajos was your sister, Louise. She dressed as a man because no woman would have been taken seriously onstage at that time in Hungary. Your father wanted to dump her into a marriage—the kitchen, the kids, et cetera. She was great for a while—compositions, concerts, critical acclaim—but the war came and you had to emigrate. That's when she got sick. MS. You tried to help her. Lifted her hands onto the piano, brought them down, and in the notes she played, more and more off-kilter, you heard the music of your rage and helplessness—and when she died it was that music you and Ferenc kept playing, disguised as cover tunes. The last night at the Palais Royale, the bad notices in the newspapers— the world walked out on her. And you've been using that music to punish us ever since.

Jakes woke in a swamp of wet clothing, the phone on his chest, buzzing. Had he called Miklós in his sleep? Jakes's hands were buried in a crack between the sofa cushions, so filled with pins and needles he dropped the phone and yelled, Fuck, and had to pick it up between his palms like a brick between plates. He used his nose to hit the answer button. Is this Lyle Jakes? The voice on the other end was female, hostile. Well, he replied, with the same hesitation he used when the bank called about his line of credit, or the hydro company about a bill, or his mother about whether he'd gotten a real job yet. Listen, asshole, I'm calling to tell you to stop leaving those fucked-up messages. Who is this? he murmured. Susan Inkster. She paused, then: He killed himself. Jakes's fingertips were still tingling, but the more he tried to massage the pins and needles from them the more the hands just seemed to transfer the numbness back and forth. She was sobbing. Couldn't you have left him alone? He was doing fine until you started pestering him. No, said Jakes, I was trying to help him. Loser attracts loser, she said. You might as well have killed him yourself.

She hung up. Jakes didn't notice. It came to him—a contraption assembling itself out of castoff parts until it shuddered into motion, smoke billowing between the spokes. It moved him into his coat, down the hall, along the sidewalk straight to Miklós's place, given wide berth by the other pedestrians frightened of his tiredness, the dreams flitting in his eyes. Blocks away he could already hear the notes dribbling from the piano—it was the ugliest sound in the world—pooling on the floor, flowing under the door, down the elevator shaft, out the foyer to the sidewalk where he waded through them upriver to the source.

Jakes put his mouth next to Miklós's keyhole. He wanted to confess all of it. There was the sound of rubbing, as if Miklós had pressed his own ear to the other side, but Jakes instead pictured the old man's mouth on the keyhole, as if Miklós was preparing to eat whatever confession Jakes made through it. Ferenc came up the steps, shuffled down the hall, and squatted beside him, his hand on Jakes's shoulder. Even shit can have its victory, the old man whispered.

Jakes remembered his roommates rolling off the bed laughing, before the medicine and liquor had hit his stomach. He'd held it in, every bit of poison, for a few more minutes of dignity. Then he'd risen into their laughter, lurched to the bathroom, gripped the seat, and thrown it all up—a mash of bile and Southern Comfort and medicine.

Another old man came down the apartment hall in a long coat and hat. He also knelt beside him and put an arm around his neck.

One of his roommates had followed him into the bathroom, told him to move from the toilet, he needed to piss. But

Jakes hadn't moved. He was blind sick, immobile, the force of the heaves sealing his eyes. He couldn't have moved if he tried.

A third old man climbed down the security ladder from the rooftop hatch, and joined the other two, knitting their arms around Jakes. A window opened at the far end of the hallway and a fourth old man climbed through awkwardly. A fifth stepped out of the elevator. A sixth could be heard beyond Miklós's door, calling from the street on the intercom. All their arms were around Jakes now, squeezing words from him like notes from an accordion.

That night at the dorm, his roommates had come into the bathroom. Jakes could hear their voices, but it was impossible to tell how many there were. Move it, loser. We need to piss. We're warning you. Jakes had raised a hand in the midst of his retching, to protest, but they'd pissed anyway. A hot ammonia rain.

The heat from the old men was like a lost warmth, Jakes was a kid in his parents' bed, the perfect heat of a perfect sleep.

He'd risen from the toilet that night long after everyone had gone, soaked in piss, heavy with all that went missing. That's what they'd counted up for him, what he now owned, his capital, and Jakes would sell it, every bit of that surplus of loss, to an unsuspecting world. He would make them pay.

Not bad, came the murmur through the door. Yep, not bad at all, echoed the old men, still squatting by Jakes, encircling him. Let's hear it for our boy, they whispered. Clap, clap, clap, is what they said, all together, using their teeth instead of their hands. Then the door opened.

A DEATH

Kate Cayley

Considering she had spent her entire career writing about sex, she had had very little of it. Reading in bed, she would feel an embarrassed juvenile resentment, as though she alone had not been invited to the party. She would rest the book on her chest for a moment, her skin dryly hot under the pages, look up at the ceiling, which was scrubbed as a blank canvas. She'd acquired a cleaning service when she turned sixty, an arch gift from Maura, who lived nearby now, with their daughter. Maura felt that too much of the housework had devolved on her when they lived together, in the days when she'd insisted to Maura that hiring a cleaning service was a betrayal of her principles. But her own work was more demanding than Maura's, and she'd been away from home so much, years of readings, sold-out lectures, her compact suitcase wheeled through airports.

That attention was fading now, she thought, absently stroking the book on her chest. Even the feminists were losing interest in her these days. There was so much to be outraged about; she could not hold their attention forever. It was disappointing.

The cleaners the agency sent did not like her. She ran her fingers along edges, told them her own grandmother had cleaned houses after coming from Corsica with nothing, though the

Corsican grandmother, whatever her sacrifices, had resulted in
a granddaughter who owned a house full of pottery and rugs.
She did not tell them about her grandmother to be friendly, or
even to establish fallacious solidarity, but to insist she deserved
what was hers. She admitted this about herself; she was honest.
She sometimes felt ashamed, in bed with the book on her
chest, a shame as abrupt and resentful as her feeling about sex,
something she would never admit to, except when alone. She
lifted the book up again.

> It is an ancient Mariner,
> And he stoppeth one of three.
> 'By thy long grey beard and glittering eye,
> Now wherefore stopp'st thou me?'

She disliked her name. Primula Chance (her mother had no
sense, and loved flowers). It was the name of a victim in a mur-
der mystery, squatting down beside a flower bed. She went by
Avery, published as P. L. Chance. She dressed in pinstripe suits,
with cufflinks, wore high-heeled leather boots. Silver shading
her eyelids, powder smoothed over her face, her eyebrows
redrawn in pencil. She thought, stepping out into the wash of
lights in a fifteen-hundred-seat lecture hall, of Bowie stepping
onstage, his easy sneer, his quality of having all the time in the
world. He was a god. She understood the need for gods. She
would not sanitize herself, not to please the feminists, not to
please anyone. She was not good at pleasing, certainly not at
pleasing Maura, who had hated the way she said *the feminists*
as if such a generalization were possible. But she couldn't help
herself and didn't want to. An old woman now, a hag, she had
surmounted any question of pleasing long ago.

When she was writing her thesis, she would visit her supervisor in his opulently smoky office (it was 1980), both of them
talking over each other. Alan Greene, white-haired, spit flying
from his mouth, cultivating vulgarity as a defense after a life-

time among polite patricians, self-conscious about his own past as a barefoot Bronx boy. These professional antagonists were, even then, mostly dead (that was growing old, she fretted, half her mind on her book, you find yourself goading antagonists who are no longer there). They had shouted at each other, slammed the desk from either side. Pens jumped. His glasses slid down his nose. He had adored her, she knew, she was one of his inaccurate enthusiasms. He was delighted by her hands, curled into fists when she wanted to emphasize a point, he put up his own fists like an indulgent grandfather.

He was also dead now. There had been a small scandal, a hand on someone's breast, not hers. He had never touched her. He had brought her for dinner at his house, his wife bending to lift a chicken from the oven, his wife was heavy and out of breath; she should have been named Primula Chance. She had cleared the plates around them while Alan lit his pipe and Avery (he did not call her Avery, he called her Chance) lit her cigarette off the last one and they argued. He had kept her from being lonely; she had been lonely everywhere else.

She joked, later on when she was famous, that she had wanted to meet a woman in a black dress and heels, but there was nothing but sensible shoes. Audiences rarely laughed, there was something sour in the joke, as she remembered the brittle puritanism of those years, the debates about pornography and representation. Her hands were always in fists. She wrote out, every morning, Thucydides's, "The society that separates its scholars from its warriors will have its thinking done by cowards and its fighting done by fools." She wanted to be a warrior for beauty, defend it from the correct and fairminded: art, she thought, had nothing to do with goodness or justice.

Maura wore a black dress and heels. She introduced Avery on a book tour, in the days when her first book was a bestseller, and she introduced her matter-of-factly, which piqued Avery's interest: she had grown used to being called inflammatory or controversial, and in certain circles this was a form of praise, which she had come to want and expect. Maura, herself a well-known journalist and much younger than Avery, recited a list of Avery's achievements, neither fawning nor with the wariness a woman like her ought to have had toward such a dubious figure. Maura was amused, cool as a statue. Much later, Maura accused Avery of seeing her only shallowly. Avery had not bothered to reply. She had revered Maura for her poise, for her lack of sentimentality, for the symmetry of her face. Avery wanted to respond to a body as she responded to art itself: shaken, wondering. To live in what Foucault's lover, after his death, had described truculently to a French newspaper as "a state of passion." She had always wanted that, even as a child, and later, shouting at Alan Greene, making him laugh until he cried, dashing tears onto the papers on his desk, saying, *Oh my dear, my dear, how will you live.* She had conceived of her life as an explosion, wrung by scrupulous and untenable devotions. Being tenable was not the point. She would be the lover as Baudelaire had understood the position, at mercy and yet at a distance. The beloved looking out a window, arranged across a bed. Maura told her once she was the only queer she'd ever met who seemed to be genuinely regretful, even to the point of seeing herself as cheated, that it was not the late eighteenth century or perhaps the early nineteenth, who wished for the electric charge of absolute secrecy. It was a fair thing to say. She would have preferred damnation to packing school lunches, fretting over appropriate socialization, the house strewn with crumbs, toys, the domestic effluvia which, seeing Alan's wife with the chicken, she'd wanted to avoid.

They named the baby Allegra. She was fourteen now. She looked like Maura and someone else, the number code they'd paid for, chosen because he was tall and working toward a PhD on Proust. Avery sometimes played with the idea that he would cross her path. Some man at a conference, traces of her daughter's face.

She was surprised to find that she adored Allegra as soon as the milky wobbly stage was over, from the moment Allegra began to speak in what were obviously words: distinct experimental sounds directed at objects, her eyes wide from the onslaught of the world.

Avery's love for Allegra had not kept Maura from leaving. Now the house was clean and quiet, and she went out only to teach, travelled only to give guest lectures, readings. Her last book had provoked enough response that her schedule was gratifyingly full. Sometimes young women yelled at her from the audience and she answered steadily in her smoker's rasp, making the women yelling seem shrilly vulnerable. She had once been notorious for storming off the stage when asked anything she regarded as a stupid question, but she had stopped when she began to feel defeated. An old woman fleeing before an invading army, her hair covered in a shawl, her few belongings wrapped in her skirt.

When Allegra was not with her she washed the dishes herself; it took too long to fill the dishwasher. She skulked through the house, leaving very little trace except in the study, in which she often ate her meals, scooping food into her mouth, trying to keep her eyes on the page or the screen. Books rose around her. The ogress in the fortress, she thought, catching sight of herself reflected in the window at night. Tomato sauce gathered in the corners of her mouth, her unprepared face slack, her thick grey hair in tufts and furrows like a neglected field of dead grass. Bits of food in her teeth. She was a ruin. It was something she relished about being alone. The luxurious privacy of her face in the window, her body revealed by the falling-open bathrobe. Her study was at the back of the house, facing a ravine. Sometimes she could hear rustlings from it, animals scuffling, bird calls.

When Allegra came, she kept the study door half-open, an ambivalent invitation. Maura said it was like Bluebeard's room. But Allegra was nothing like the gullible young wife. She had the level-headedness of an intelligent, beloved only daughter of divorced parents who knew themselves to be important figures in the world. Avery at that age had been grasping, furiously curious, sure of herself but not as Allegra was. She stood very straight, played the oboe, wore tooled leather cuffs on each wrist, her neck wound with a baroque arrangement of chains and pendants, each one representing a friendship or something she believed to be true. She seemed to Avery to have no need to press her advantage or to raise her voice. She knew the names of painters and composers, and Maura provided her with curated experiences of her birth country and a series of other countries. She was accomplished and pristine, like a twenty-first-century version of a girl at a finishing school, only her conversation was wider, she was frank about sex, gender, politics, while treating all these things as not really very serious, when to Avery and Maura they were deadly serious, enough to shout at each other about.

On this visit, she found Allegra sitting in her chair at her desk, half-watching the screen, not thinking she was somewhere she should not be (this was something that fascinated Avery, the extent to which Allegra thought nothing was forbidden, the world before her endlessly available, even losing lustre because of it, like the dispiriting effect of a room full of unwrapped presents). She'd knocked over a pile of books, and one of her bare feet was resting on Avery's *Art, Sex, and Nihilism: 1700–2000*.

"What are you doing?"

"Watching YouTube."

"Where's your phone?"

"Maura took it."

"Why did your mother take it?"

"My mother," she said, sweetly imitating Avery, "took it because I was spending too much time on YouTube."

Allegra turned away, smiling slightly, knowing Avery could not resist anything that felt like subversion, even when it served no obvious end (Maura had wanted to know why it was so important to adopt the opposing stance, even if it was meaningless, even if it made Avery appear belligerent or vindictive; Avery replied that that was the point of freedom, that it was useless and for its own sake and Maura told her she was impossible to live with). Avery resettled the pile of books and sat on it, beside Allegra. They were heavy books, and she wondered if Allegra had knocked them over on purpose. The thought pleased her.

It was late afternoon in late September, the day cloudy, branches writhing in the wind. The animals in the ravine would take cover, burrow into their holes. She'd planned to take Allegra out for dinner. She watched a cardboard box skid along the road outside, the smell of approaching rain coming from the open window, and thought they'd order takeout instead, maybe she'd make Allegra sit through an old movie. *The Birds, Vertigo.*

"You're not watching," Allegra said.

"Should I be?"

"Yeah, this one's good."

A young woman shimmered into view, singing so rapidly it was difficult to make out words, the camera lingering on her face. She was in a white room, and her face was painted white; only her hair, which was severely black, separated it from the walls.

"Who is that? Who is that?"

"It's Cecile," Allegra said, smiling. "You like it? Some of my friends don't, but I think she's so good. She's from France I think, like, a small town in France? But she lives in Brooklyn now."

They watched *Vertigo*, open containers of sushi drying out in front of them, Avery thinking of the woman's forbidding, delicate face, Allegra draped in blankets, surprisingly fascinated. The rain drilled at the house.

"How can he not *know* it's her? It obviously is," Allegra said, shifting toward the screen as Kim Novak reappeared as a salesgirl, concealed in crass makeup.

"It's a Freudian metaphor," Avery answered, and Allegra threw a pillow at her, laughing, showing the newly liberated row of her straightened teeth.

"Don't patronize me, Avery!"

"How am I patronizing you?"

"You know."

"No. Tell me."

"You're doing it again."

She threw another pillow, more forcefully this time, still smiling, but it had become the smile of a person trying to show she was not hurt. After the film had ended and Allegra was in her room, reading something for school (Avery had asked what, and Allegra had shifted the book so the cover wasn't visible from the doorway, said, *It doesn't matter*), Avery sat in her study and considered (she was not as quick as she thought, some things came too late) that Allegra had wanted something else, and it made her feel her failure.

She'd taught Allegra to call her by her first name, saying it was an ideological affectation to insist that a child had two mothers. She would allow herself to be Allegra's other parent (as the birth certificate, post-adoption, allowed), but not her mother. Now she sometimes longed to have been more compromising, seeing the ease with which other children, the children of Maura's friends, used the title interchangeably for their parents. Avery wondered if Allegra had wished for less insistence on acknowledging construction. Avery should have lived it more; it made it difficult now to tell Allegra how much she loved her, and she had not provided the conditions that could have made Allegra certain of that without it needing to be said.

She typed *Cecile*.

The face was absurdly proportioned, reminding her of the kitsch sold in Catholic stores that carried christening robes, dresses, and little shiny grey suits for first communions, displayed among crinkling eruptions of dull pink or ochre cellophane. She'd been measured for a dress, looked away when her mother saw her eyeing the suits, pretended to be interested in promises of those little net bags of enameled pink candies. Statuary of the Virgin rising around her. She looked at the dozens of Virgins with their painted mouths and rolling eyes and felt a stirring, not desire yet, not at seven, but longing for something she could not give a name to.

She wrote on the notepad beside her keyboard: *iconography of Catholic martyrdom resurgent in YouTube celebrity.*

She spent more time online than she would have admitted if anyone asked. At first, she'd been contemptuous, a contempt that masked unease, knowing that once she succumbed the fascination would be too great, which was true. Maura used the possibilities (of communication, of surveillance) as tools: she was not troubled by them, and did not let them take up too much of her time. Allegra had gone to a daycare that had a webcam so parents could watch their children. When they were both working from home Maura would call her over, make her hover behind Maura's swivel chair and watch the slightly blurred image of Allegra, self-possessed even then, stacking wooden blocks, painting in watercolour, her tongue poking up to lick snot from her upper lip, unaware that she was being watched. Avery hated it, feeling they were disturbing Allegra's rights, like government representatives of healthy development.

Now the world online beckoned, more glittering and lawless and interestingly disgusting than anything she could have imagined.

Cecile, she discovered, was twenty-seven, a performance artist and painter as well as a singer, identified as gender-fluid but used a female pronoun, and lived alone.

Avery only realized how long she'd been sitting in the chair, the voice washing over her, emerging from that cold small face, when she looked up and saw the sky, leaching out into grey outside her window. There was a crick in her neck, her mouth acrid. She shook her head, amazed at how easy it was and wondering at herself for not knowing this before. A state of passion, the object perfect and untouchable.

The weekend was over. Allegra kissed her cheek and climbed into Maura's car. Maura lingered, standing on the front steps of the house she'd lived in for fifteen years. She wore a wide-brimmed hat as though she did not want to be recognized.

"How are you?" she asked Avery, tentatively enough to show she thought she was not well.

"Fine. I'm fine. Busy."

Avery held the screen door open behind her.

"Dinner for Allegra's birthday?"

The ritual dinner in the farm-to-table restaurant they had taken her to since she was eight, showing off her good manners, always the only person in the place younger than thirty. More recently showing off their own goodwill, their tense civility.

"If I have to."

"Jesus, Avery, you don't make anything easy."

Allegra leaned on the car horn, just one blast. The noise covered whatever it was Maura said next.

"What was that?"

"Nothing. See you Friday."

As Avery closed the door, she considered the possibilities. Maura's mouth had barely moved. She could have said anything. *I never want to see you again. I miss you.* Avery locked the door behind her and fell asleep on the couch.

She was not saving herself for anything, and ideas of prudence or caution made her think of her dead grandmother, crossing herself, counting her money into a shoebox, a miser of the heart. Avery squandered her time and her attention. She memorized all of Cecile's lyrics, read blogs and message boards analyzing her use of harpsichord, harp, violin, debating references in the songs to various mythologies, references to the singer's own life, her difficult upbringing, her break from her parents, her move to America, her erratic behaviour at concerts. She was given to cryptic statements, claims of supernatural insight, sometimes wept during interviews, or refused to speak at all. Avery believed that Cecile knew, as Avery knew, that her purpose was to be infuriating, obscene, obscure, misdirecting. Avery (usually very late at night) convinced herself that Cecile was anticipating and amplifying her own scholarship. She even began preparing a series of lectures, though she never got past notes. Anyway, there was still the book tour to get through. She was tired, leaned her head down on her desk, jerked up again as the next song began, the video that showed Cecile crowd-surfing in a vast black space, only her figure illuminated, glowing in her red dress, a sea of hands surging beneath her, arms swarming out of the darkness, apparently unattached to bodies. Cecile held Avery's eyes cannily, and Avery whispered the words under her breath, as though someone would hear her.

Rising from the chair, Avery barely kept her balance. Shook her head. *You old fool.*

The leaves turned. She had lunch with Maura to discuss money, schedules. They sat across from each other at a table by the window, the weak sunlight blanching Maura's face. Avery kept her chair in the shadow. She'd allowed the hairdresser to dye her hair, though she hadn't gone as far as her original brown, more an artful spacing out of different shades, but the effect was blunter than she'd wanted.

"You look like Cruella De Vil."

"Is that a compliment?"

Maura reached across the table. Avery moved her hand away.

"Allegra says you have a new interest."

"Yes. I'm thinking of a book."

"Aren't you always."

There was another silence, and this time Avery opened her hand, half-hoping Maura would take it, but Maura leaned forward and lifted a thick piece of artificially iron-grey hair, tucked it behind Avery's ear.

"I liked it better before."

In the restaurant bathroom, Avery examined herself in the mirror, untucked the strand. In the pot-lights of the bathroom, her face was drained, her hair expensively unconvincing. She grimaced, ridiculous, warned.

The New York lecture was sold out. She stood, two weeks after the restaurant, again in front of the mirror, the clothes she'd worn on the plane kicked into a corner. Perhaps the lighting was better here; she felt invigorated, smoothed the lapels of her silvery suit. She was going to enjoy this. There had been credible death threats, which meant security, police presence. She marched onto the stage, gripped the lectern like a pulpit, did not refer to notes, kept her chin up, let her voice rise at anticipated challenges. The applause was punctuated by shouting, stamping feet, which could have been approbation or protest but either way meant success.

Questions were limited to fifteen minutes, moderated by her introducer, an essayist she hadn't heard of. The woman barely concealed her dislike, and had obviously agreed to introduce her in order to prove a point about her own commitment to open debate. It was possible she wished she'd had second thoughts, and was now attempting to demonstrate, a little hysterically, her allegiances. Avery was braced for that; she would have felt she'd gone soft if the note of derision was not there. Avery silently accused the introducer of all kinds of things: a trust fund, environmental sensitivities, persecution complexes. Her inability to resist caricaturing anyone who disagreed with her was one of the reasons Maura had left. But

Maura couldn't know how frightened she was of the crowd, no longer enraged but laughing. If she could keep them angry, they would not laugh.

"One more question," the moderator said.

The questioner was a small woman, dressed with the unfussy neatness of a teacher who liked good clothes: white loose blouse with a lace collar, navy blue skirt, little cloth shoes that reminded Avery of the worker's slippers her own generation had worn to show affinity with Mao, one of the many things she hoped her peers now thought of with shame. There was a green ribbon tied around the woman's neck. It was the ribbon that made Avery recognize her, even before she spoke; once she spoke Avery could feel the ripple of interest in the audience, a few whispers. She forced herself to listen closely, something she was bad at, and not be distracted by the miracle.

The green ribbon, Avery knew, was a nod to Cecile's obsession with the folk tale of the man who marries a girl with a green ribbon around her neck, which he unties on the wedding night. His bride's head rolls onto the floor.

There was a song about it. Avery knew all the words. It was twenty minutes long, sung from the point of view of the woman, hoping someone will untie the green ribbon.

"I don't have a question," Cecile said, bowing her head toward the microphone, clutching it in her left hand. "I just wanted to tell you that I have admiration for your work. You offered me a way to think about my life as artifice, which has been very valuable to me."

It would have been usual to end this with thanks, but Cecile abruptly handed the microphone back and sat down. Her sense of her own consequence was so great that thanks was not in order. If anything, she was the one conferring a favour. Avery would have expected nothing less.

"Are you coming?" the moderator said. The lecture hall was empty, some of the chairs askew. Glossy cardstock flyers for the next lecture (Public Portraits, Public Provocations: a series) left on the seats or the floor. Avery got up stiffly, and the moderator moved away, through the tall black doors to their left, assuming she was following. Avery held her hand up to shield herself from the glare of the lights, her other hand pressed to the knot in her back. She was alone. A bundle of sticks, shrunken in the grey suit. Dry bones.

No, not alone. Someone was in the far doorway, waiting. The person, seeing her look, walked into the light and along the aisle, stopped a few feet away.

"Come and talk to me," Cecile said.

They went to a restaurant next door, Avery ignoring her phone, which bloomed with messages; the driver had arrived to take her back to her hotel.

White tables, white chairs, the bar topped with granite, the floor polished concrete, pitted in places to emulate stone, the walls rising grey, becoming glass that curved into the ceiling, the city outside as mysterious and neutral as the view from a plane. Cecile led her to the bar, where they perched on white cylinders. Avery felt ungainly, her legs only just reaching the floor, pressing the toes of her boots down hard. With anyone else she would have demanded to go elsewhere, but she thought that if she asked for anything Cecile would vanish, like in a folk tale. Cecile slouched with her legs crossed under her on the stool. She looked at Avery shyly, ducking her head as she had at the microphone, the shyness calculated. Her artificiality ran so deep it was sincere. Avery's eyes filled with tears.

Thinking about it the next morning, Avery knew she'd talked too much. Cecile sat very still, tipping her head back to sip her first, second, and third gin. She had not seemed to mind. It was praise, elaborately phrased, abject. She must have known no greater love. Avery's eyes kept filling with tears. Cecile looked away as Avery patted her cheeks with the napkin as impersonally as she could. She thought of Alan Greene wiping his eyes: *My dear, my dear, how will you live.* She did not know how she had lived. Cecile watched her over the rim of the glass. She drank the gin straight. It was some kind of expensive infusion, deep yellow, reminding Avery of cat piss. When Cecile finished the third she put the glass down hard on the bar so it cracked, not shattering but dividing neatly along the bottom like an opening fault line.

"It took me a long time to learn to do that," she said, looking over at the bartender, whose back was turned. "You'll pay for me?" she asked, getting up.

"Are you going?"

"It's late." She pointed outside. The city had not dimmed, but the firmness of the gesture convinced Avery it was the middle of the night. She almost expected to find the bartender gone, the doors locked.

She held out her hand. Cecile did not take it.

"It's nice how much you love me," she said.

"I do. I do."

Cecile lifted her hand to the ribbon.

"I'd like you to keep this."

Avery waited.

"Take it," Cecile said impatiently.

She waited another moment, not sure she had understood. Still unsure, she touched the ribbon, not the taut loop around Cecile's neck, just the loose end that fell to her collarbone.

"Come on. What will happen?" Cecile said, and Avery thought of the head on the floor. It seemed possible. She had imagined, or wished for, things like that. The things that really happened were disappointing.

"Don't be afraid," Cecile said, and she was soft now; Avery reached clumsily for the ribbon. It slid off and then she had it in her hands. Cecile stepped back. There was a pink mark where the ribbon had been; she'd cinched it tight.

"Thank you," Avery said, looking down at the limp ribbon.

"You're welcome," Cecile said, and left, her little shoes slapping on the concrete floor.

Avery saw herself reflected in the mirror behind the bar. The bartender was gone. The mirror wavered. She was an old woman. The crowd was laughing. They howled laughter. She did not run. She stood, hearing the laughter grow like an echo in a canyon, lifting her arms to receive it. She held the green ribbon as high as she could so that the tips waved in the push of air from the silent blades of the enormous ceiling fan, which hung above her as though she were in the pathway of a propeller plane. The room shook with laughter and Avery, unafraid, waved the ribbon in the air.

The bartender had stepped out for a cigarette and to breathe the night air and crane her neck up at the buildings (she had lived in New York for years, but she could still feel wonder). When she came back inside and saw Avery standing with the ribbon over her head she asked her if she was okay, and Avery caught sight of her own face in the window and resolved never to wear such a dark shade of lipstick again and felt mocked by Cecile and the bartender and when the bartender asked her again if she was okay Avery rushed out and walked all the way to the hotel, and the next morning the sun was warm on her face as the plane rose and she felt for the green ribbon in her purse.

She had a heart attack in her sleep three months later. When Allegra and Maura sorted through Avery's things Allegra discovered a sheaf of handwritten notes about the evening in the bar, tied up by the green ribbon in an uncharacteristically bathetic gesture, and slid them into her own bag. Maura kept excusing herself to go to the bathroom, where she sat on the edge of the tub and sobbed, and when she came back Allegra didn't tell her about the pages and the ribbon. Allegra disliked the way Maura's violent grief took over everything, and even constructed a private fiction in which Avery would not have died if Maura had not left her. Allegra was romantic, underneath her composure. Because of this, she kept the pages to herself. The notes were about that phantom laughter, about the fear of being laughed at, which astonished Allegra because she was still too young to understand that adults were undefended, coming as she did from two people with magnificent defenses.

(Cecile did not hear about Avery's death for months. The day after the lecture she travelled to Vermont, where she recorded a new album in a renovated monastery. When recording she stayed offline. It's possible that when she did hear of it, it did not affect her very much. Allegra, reading Avery's words, wondered about this, about how much or how little someone like Cecile considered the rest of the world, when not in her line of vision, to actually exist. Allegra listened to Cecile's music for years, wondering about her, thinking about the death and the imaginary laughter, thinking about her mother loving Cecile, who seemed, as Allegra grew older, to be embalmed by her own efforts in the petulant grief and self-regard of youth. Allegra, who becomes a lawyer focusing on women's rights, finds Cecile embarrassing, a sign of all the ways in which Avery had been mistaken.

Allegra wears the ribbon from time to time. Not around her neck, that would be too much. Tied around her forearm, pushed up, concealed by her loose sleeve. She doesn't tie it in a bow, she crosses it around and around, knotting it just above her wrist, the tight loops pressing into her skin like the sandal straps of Greek soldiers, shown on ceremonial urns, marching into battle.)

NEKA

Naomi Fontaine

Translated from the French by Kathryn Gabinet-Kroo

Sitting beside her, I casually take her hand. It's veiny, brown, small, and gentle. I look at my own, which would be almost identical to hers if I didn't paint my nails with deep purple polish. And if my palms were smoother. Maybe time softens skin, the way age softens the look in someone's eyes.

My mother doesn't talk much about her childhood. When she does, it's always about the meals. She says, "There were no vegetables, no fruit, we ate noodles all the time. I used to go to my older sister's place to drink cow's milk, we didn't have any at home." She says "cow's milk" and it makes me laugh. I wouldn't dare ask what kind of milk she drank at her house. She finds it amusing. Sort of the same way I find having had to wear my sisters' hand-me-downs laughable. It won't kill you.

I try to imagine what this reserve looked like. A poor village, inhabited by poor people, who survived on sacks of potatoes and flour. How she must have felt when she had to sleep with her sisters, three in a bed. The minuscule assortment of flower-patterned dishes, little plates, and a teapot, reappearing at Christmas, year after year, the cherished artifacts from her youth.

Her father worked hard for the city, building new infrastructures. For a meagre wage, as meagre as the slices of meat that he alone ate when the family sat down for supper. This man of few words, my grandfather, had seen the draconian changes in his community. Like all the others of his generation, he had settled his brood in a modest wood cabin. He then made up his mind that he would not moulder away in his makeshift shelter. Resilient, he did his forty hours a week. He told his daughters to go to school even though he could neither read nor write. And although he couldn't give them steak to eat very often, no one would ever go hungry.

He was a visionary, a man capable of understanding the path his world was taking and so chose to follow it.

In the boxes piled up at the back of my mother's closet, I find an Indian outfit, straight out of an old western. There's a leather vest. The artisan had embroidered an owl on the back and adorned the front with fringe. The skirt, made of matching fabric, looked more like a Hawaiian hula skirt with its layers of fringe than the skirts worn by our ancestors, had they actually worn skirts, those Amazons whom I pictured as being as strong as men.

"My mother had sewn for us, for my twin and me, traditional clothes to wear when we started high school," she explains. "We went to the White people's school. Can you imagine how ashamed I was to wear that outfit? Dead. I'd rather have been dead."

Years later, during my last year of high school, a show had been planned as part of a fundraising campaign for the school I was attending. I offered to participate. I was going to do a traditional dance to a popular Innu song. And I chose that very costume for my performance. I had added little bits of metal to the fringes on the skirt. With each step, you could hear a soft jingling that caught everyone's attention. I swanned around, my flushed cheeks burning, thrilled to have everyone's eyes on me.

It's impossible to imagine my mother without her faith. I was very young when I learned what faith was: believing in something you do not see. We were little, so we followed her into this church that looked more like a community hall than a sacred place, with neither bell tower nor statues. A modern cement building next to a bowling alley, it had small windows on the sides but no stained glass. It did have a big wooden door to welcome the believers, who arrived on Sunday, wearing their finest attire, a Bible in hand.

Many memories spill from those doors. The people sang loudly, clapping their hands and smiling broadly. They knelt, they implored. They raised their hands to the heavens and were sometimes moved to tears.

Admitting to being a member of the Protestant Church had created a total scandal in the family and on the reserve.

Since colonization and the missionaries, and despite the boarding schools, in our villages, it was all about the Catholic religion. Since the Innu were very spiritual beings and likely to believe in things beyond their perception, they did not find Catholicism distasteful. Suffering the misery of famines and arid winters and exhausted from battling the forest, they had accepted the idea that there was a higher power. My mother was the first to rebel, the first not to have her children baptized. The first to stay away from religious ceremonies, first communions, novenas and recitations of the rosary. She was not yet twenty. She hadn't been tortured, at least not physically.

There is an Innu word for Protestants like my mother. They're called *kamatau-aiamiat*, "those who pray in a strange way." You have to understand the rejection, the exclusion that comes of not belonging to the majority's religion. It was an insult in the eyes of a very observant people. I can't talk about her without talking about her fearlessness.

Faith is something that I have. Believing in something beyond what my eyes can see. Especially when I'm sad, especially when I'm fragile, especially when I fail to understand this unjust, cruel life that spares criminals but scorns peace-loving mothers. I believe that there is something greater than this life, but if I'm wrong and everything that exists can be seen, at least throughout my life, I'll have had hope.

Her decision to leave the reserve had surprised me one spring. We were so young, scarcely old enough to handle our boredom in the back of the big, garish green Aerostar, but we tried our best to keep still for the interminable ten-hour drive from Uashat to Quebec City. We laughed ourselves silly that day, until our jaws ached, until my mother got annoyed and threatened to stop the van by the side of the road and punish us severely.

Was she escaping? Expressing a desire long repressed? Was it the culmination of a process undertaken some years earlier? Or the tentative hope that things would be better somewhere else?

I often asked myself that question. Why go so far away, when everything that belonged to us could be found in Uashat? She enrolled me in a private high school, one of the most prestigious in the city, because I'd received good grades in elementary school. Fine, except that no one had prepared me for that environment.

My friends' fathers were lawyers, professors, company presidents. My own father had foolishly died in a car accident. I was out of my league. Their mothers supervised their households and their children's schoolwork. I pictured them as very chic women, sipping a cup of hot tea as they waited for their guests in the living room. They cooked shark with tartar sauce for dinner and folded the laundry. Such women did not laugh uproariously, they crossed their legs at the knee when they sat. I did not come from the same stock. We ate shepherd's pie and macaroni with meat. Friday was fast food night. On Sunday, we had the best meal of the week—roast chicken or steak, and mashed potatoes. There was always something for dessert.

During that whole time, between the meals and the whimsical organization of a family with five children, my mother studied. I saw her in the evening, after supper, at the huge kitchen table that she used as a desk, reading and rereading her notes from class. Closing her eyes, reciting them by heart. Memorization I now know, serves no purpose. And so I find her single-parent reality even sadder. Like a form of torment, a hardship. It is impossible to talk about my mother without talking about her strength.

She sleeps at my place on Mondays, in my four-room apartment with bath, which overflows with toys and novels to be read. She borrows my son's room, which is in perpetual disorder. She doesn't pay it any attention. She tickles his neck, his thighs, his ribs, his back, until he squeals for her to stop. Close to tears, he begs for more, until it's time for bed. We often pray, to give thanks and ask for the courage to face another day.

Late at night, she holds a cup of hot water in her hand, and we sit like two close friends as she tells me about her work as advocate at the Uauitshitun health and social services centre. For several years, she has spent her time meeting young people, the older ones and the not-so-old. These are the defeated, the broken, those close to collapse. Their faces bear witness to a heavy, unassuaged sorrow. Completely overwhelmed, they show up one Monday, with a tiny glimmer of hope. She sees them at the very beginning of their recovery. This woman—who became a mother very young, who lived with her big brood of kids in a house provided by the council, who was worn down by problems with money and men—this woman is the ear that listens, counsels, tries to understand, once a week, offering a helping hand in the form of a coffee.

One winter evening, she is exhausted. She cries. My mother's tears, as rare as they are unbearable, reminded me of a child's. Big tears, held back for so long, slide down her cheeks, and her weeping dissolves into the silence of my apartment. Awkwardly, I put a hand on her arm and she immediately pulls it away. She does not want to be consoled; she just needs to let it out, to give free rein to her immense sorrow. At last, she tells me, "I know they don't trust me. My colleagues. They look at me with suspicion, as if I wanted to harm them. And that, my girl, is the worst thing of all."

I understand only too well that feeling, as old as the hills, of not measuring up. It's not that she does not want, it's that she wants for everyone. Her years of exile taught her a certain discipline. Being able to count only on herself, she created herself out of the sacred bonds of single parenthood. She fought, and she will continue to fight throughout her life. A mother bear.

A few weeks later, she tells me that she has enrolled in a master's program. I'm surprised, since I'd always thought of her as an unconventional woman. She'd been working just a few short years in a field that seemed to enthrall her, judging from the projects that she organized and to which she was deeply committed. Then, with no feeling other than that her work was done, she decided to study other things that, at first glance, seemed unnecessary but that would apparently take her further, higher. While most people walk, stagnate, wander around in circles, I had the impression that she was running. Running toward herself.

As an adult, caught between a rock and a hard place, I strive to be a woman, with all my faults, transgressions, and penchants for futile endeavours. But also with the simple dignity that comes of being this woman's daughter.

That's where I fell asleep the first time, Neka. Round head, fists like two big marbles. Eyes closed. Your skin as soft and sweet as water. Mine all red and swollen. Barely enough breath to cry. Only the desire to snuggle up close. That's where I slept, between the hollow of your shoulder and the heat of your chest.

THE TEST

David Bezmozgis

Maybe you met through an app. Maybe you liked one of his photos, or he liked one of yours. The one at the gym. The one by the lake. The one with the dog. In a group with boisterous, assorted others, to indicate the bright fulsomeness of your life. Or in an exotic locale: beside a camel, astride an elephant, amidst penguins.

Maybe you were introduced through friends. Because you should really really meet.

Maybe you knew each other before, when this wasn't possible, and the memory of the other, like a dormant, red-tipped cinder, has flared into a flame.

Maybe this was preceded by a lot of texting: playful, teasing, or sincere.

Maybe there were emails. Maybe there were even, for reasons of circumstance and romance, postmarked handwritten letters.

Maybe you have FaceTimed or Zoomed. Maybe you have exchanged spontaneous or artful pics. Or innocent and endearing ones from childhood. Or others bolder, carnal, so graphically personal as to be impersonal.

Maybe you agreed to meet first at a café, or in a park, or you went for a walk in some eclectic, self-regarding part of the city. Maybe you wore your masks. Maybe you took them off. Maybe you detected but dismissed some discongruity. Maybe you brought along your dog as a reliable arbiter.

Maybe you were cautious, loath to rush into anything. Maybe you had learned the hard way. Maybe you had been hurt too many times before. Or once very badly. Or only very recently. Maybe you promised yourself that, this time, you would break the intractable pattern and learn from your mistakes. Maybe you promised your friends, your relatives, your therapist, the mystical power to which you turned when the remorseless black emptiness cast you mute and immobile.

Maybe you were eager, heedless. Maybe you had been alone too long. Maybe you had tired of your meekness, your fearfulness, your uncertainty. Maybe you needed to be touched. Maybe you could no longer recognize yourself and the lonely trek your life had become. Maybe you wanted something cool and transitory, a ripple on the surface, a pulse of light, a clear high chime. Or maybe you wanted consumption, immolation, to strip away a layer of skin.

Maybe you agreed to go to his place. Maybe you invited him to yours. Maybe you hesitated out front, or when the elevator came, or at the threshold, where you glanced discreetly over your shoulder. Maybe you were smiling, nervously, giddily, partaking of the joke that is two strangers on the cusp.

Maybe none of this bears repeating. Maybe it's an old and tired story. Maybe it's merely gossip, prurience. Or a swirl of chemicals. Or it works only counterintuitively. Maybe it starts to die once he opens his fridge, or you go use the toilet. When you look at his bookshelves, or when he fails to look at yours. Or maybe there's just enough. Or it's down to sunk costs. Or you're pathologically curious, and it's that cloying, sinister, sharp-toothed urge.

But if you make it this far, it's inevitable. It's the way of the world now. So maybe you broach the subject, or maybe he does. Or maybe it's just tacit, a mutual acknowledgement of what comes next. Maybe you agree to do it simultaneously. Or maybe you make it a game: who will go first? Maybe it still feels strange and self-conscious, or ironically lewd. Maybe it still can't be done without laughing. He licks his stem with his tongue, you put yours in your mouth, or you spit on each other's, secreting that unseemly word.

Then you're consigned to waiting. Maybe you get a napkin or a plate and lay the two stems upon it, side by side, so they look like lovers in the winnowing silence after the act. Maybe he pours wine, or you mix a drink—a negroni, a cosmopolitan, an old fashioned—to give you something to do with your hands, like an actor in need of business, to calm the nerves or temper excitement. Then you stand at the kitchen counter, or sit the appropriate distance apart, the dog curled up on the floor between you. And the quality of time is different now. It feels delicate, friable. Like the wrong look, the wrong gesture, might shatter it. It could be time, or it could be you. Distinctions are hazier now.

And maybe you fix on a point on the familiar or unfamiliar floor, or the familiar or unfamiliar wall, or some part of him that is probably not his eyes, and allow yourself to conjecture, to brush your palm against the smooth basalt of your desire, to hear the echo of the ancient verse, *I am my beloved's and my beloved is mine*, to be maudlin, heart-foolish, to think inwardly what nobody is permitted to say outwardly. What if you hear the proselytizing of all the shitty love songs? What if the feeling is so vast that another person is hardly even necessary? And the room bends, water spills over the lip of the tub, the windows blow open. What if you hold very still and command him to hold very still because there are motion detectors for bad thoughts?

Because it isn't a secret, and it has never been a secret. From time immemorial, long before there was a test, these have been the options:

Neither of you is sick.
One of you is sick.
You are both sick.

ODDSMAKING

Omar El Akkad

Three times the fire had come for him, but three times he lived. First in Daughter Paradise, when he was a child, still unaccustomed to the relentless want of burning. What he remembers of that day now is the sight of the abandoned vineyards past the edge of town, high orange curls sprouting out the tops of sheds and the old tasting room. The whole of the world in the rear-view mirror of the speeding truck, muddled and half-melting: the way heat turns the image of a landscape watery, makes a still thing jitter. He remembers the sound his baby sister made next to him in the truck bed, cooing at the amber tendrils in the sky, the script of some strange and violent cursive, and his mother in whispered conversation with someone who wasn't there—*to whom God's love commits thee here, to whom God's love commits thee here*—as the town disappeared under black smoke.

Fire does this, he learned, brings out the supplicant in all things.

Twice more it came for him, in his early adulthood, during the seasons he spent scabbing on the towers while the firewatchers' union held out for a better deal. Back then the unionists used to crawl around the frontier with their brushcutters, cutting the power lines and snapping the satellite phone antennas, and sometimes a scab might go days or weeks unable to check in with the ranger's office. It happened to him the summer UC-72 tore through the northwestern edge of the valley, and by the time he caught sight of the plume churning out of Butte Creek, the fire had already rendered the sole logging road impassable. And so he ran blind through the brush and past the last standing redwoods and into the river. A year later it would happen again near the place where Bowler Camp used to be, and once again he'd escape but not undamaged. For the rest of his life he'd suffer from corseted lungs and carry a smooth pink scar that ran from his left shoulder down to his wrist. But he lived. It meant something, to live.

The betting house overlooked the old county road that connected the valley towns to Bald Eagle Mountain. Once, when the burning season was still a passing thing, millions lived in this part of the country, but now only a few thousand stubbornly held on—loggers and ruin-looters and those who remembered what it had once been like and those who believed against all reason that it would be that way again and those who chose to take their chances in the forest rather than the camps or the factories. Without judgment, the betting house served them all. It was a pretty A-frame cabin in the style of the old national park guide houses, dolled up along its road-facing side with a gaudy neon sign that flickered in electric pink: ACTION.

Worm liked to get to the betting house around dawn, when it was still quiet. Although the marks usually started to line up outside around ten in the morning, the book didn't officially open till noon, and before then the only sound in the office was that of the spinning desk fans and the papers and maps rustling. It calmed him, this partway quiet, allowed him to do his work.

It was a common misconception that his job was to pick winners or losers, towns that were most or least likely to burn.

Even some of the marks who'd been throwing their pay-cheques away at the betting house for decades still heckled him in the bar some nights when he'd failed to put an obvious burn site up on the board. *Hey, Worm, how'd you go and miss that one? Don't your bum arm tingle with the wind or some shit? Don't you see the future?*

What they didn't understand was that the house never made money on clear winners or losers. His job was to find the coin-toss towns, the places just as likely to burn as survive. That was the action that got the marks excited, sent them arguing in the hall in wild disagreement as to whether the smart money would take the over or the under. The only thing the house liked better than coin-toss towns was miraculous ones—places that seemed well out of harm's way but ended up burning, or places that stood right at the mouth of a fire but for some reason were spared. These were the picks that brought in big money—it was betting-house tradition that every odds-maker be nicknamed after the town that brought in the biggest haul at the book, and these coin-toss towns were the picks that more often than not earned an oddsmaker his name.

Worm arrived at the betting house earlier than usual, the sun still pale and shadowed behind the blue-capped mountains. He unlocked the rear door and entered the office and turned on the lights. It was a cramped room made more so by the huge Remington safe and the row of filing cabinets in which the house kept six months' of past betting records. Like the smoke from countless fires over the years, the smell of old paper permeated the walls, permeated everything.

He sat at his desk and checked the notes the overnight boy had left in the ledger, dispatches and updates from the watchtowers out near Pious and Elder and Graze Valley, the frontier places: At around midnight the watcher in Melford had reported UC-188 curling back on itself, thinning a little under an unexpected burst of rain. Fifty miles west, UC-192 was spreading east and north, threatening to jump the river.

Quietly he marked these updates down on the massive wall map behind him. It was a chaotic thing, disfigured beyond all recognition with scribbled and pinned notes, crudely redrawn borders, lines in red indicating what the fire had taken and lines in blue indicating what it might take and lines in purple indicating where his predictions had come true; wind markers and elevation markers, weather reports and satellite photos of the earth and the clouds and printed reports from the factfinders the government sent in to every obliterated town, reports that served as proof these places had really burned, proof the house had paid out fairly.

From the overnight reports and radar maps he began sketching the flight path of the fire tearing through the southern end of the valley. In government parlance they were called Uncontrolled Conflagrations but everyone in the betting house called them birds. Once there had been a fire season but now the year was the season and the migrations constant. For the last three days UC-196 had been moving northward, feeding on brushland and the places where the state hadn't sent the prisoner crews to clear the ground fuel in time. But overnight the heat dome had lifted and in its place a southern chinook had come rushing down the mountainside and he began to think the bird might double back, might change its mind.

He picked up the radio and dialed Pine County Tower 18, which stood about halfway between the fire's southern border and the small drywash towns at the very edge of the valley. A squawk of static beat back the quiet of the room and then faded.

"How you doing, Bryce?"

He cleared his throat. "I'm all right, Ruby. How you doing?"

"You think it's coming back, don't you?"

"Just tell me what you're looking at," he said.

"'Bout seventy-five miles upland, bubble clouds, slow-moving. Nothing between us but drybed and already eaten forest. I just don't see it turning, Bryce."

He didn't like the sound of his given name, had grown used to Worm over the years. But it was only two who called him Bryce anymore. He tapped the map with his marker, little red dots piling like measles on the skin of the outskirts towns. It was a kind of blindness, to be of these places, to come from the crucible of the continent, to not know any other way of living but this. Down to a man the marks who frequented the betting house talked of what they'd do when they finally hit it big and each one said they'd finally get the hell out fire country, buy a nice big house in the northern Midwest or maybe even Canada, but to a man he knew they'd always stay here. It was imprinted on them, the building and fleeing and rebuilding, the smoke-blindered life. They were as newborn animals to whom the first sight is mother and the first they'd ever seen was fire.

"Listen, do me a favour and close up shop," he said into the handset. "Hitch a ride out to 19 or 21, just till mid-week."

"You a ranger boss now?"

"Just go on, all right?"

Ruby sighed. "All right, Bryce. All right."

He set the radio down and sat awhile listening to the tongue-click sound the fans made as they turned. The other day one of the sunfarm grunts had said the temperature in Furnace Creek pushed past one-fifty though you couldn't really get a reliable read these days, and anyway so long as it's dry your body don't go full helpless. He liked that phrase. It sounded liberating, a body going full helpless.

At ten on the dot the Captain arrived. He was a brittle-looking man, scrawny but what the marks would call soft-lived, with a full head of hair and pristine Chiclets teeth even as he pushed eighty.

"Mornin', Worm," he said, shuffling over to the house safe.

"Mornin', boss."

"What's the story of the world today, Worm?"

He'd earned the nickname years earlier when he picked, while still an apprentice, UC-71 to eat up a place called

93

Wormwood. It was a line no other house in the state was offering, a town high up the mountainside, just a day removed from rain and against the prevailing wind, a born loser. But he'd seen something in the satellite photos, a buildup of fuel and the cloud cover thinning, and the Captain, who was comfortable enough to entertain the occasional bout of recklessness, let the pick stand. No sooner did Wormwood go up on the big board than every mark in the county was lined up to take the under. By the time the book closed there wasn't enough cash in the safe for the house to cover the bets, and it seemed the fire could not possibly move so far by midnight. Then at dusk, purely by chance, a rolling storm set off a batch of lightning burns that quickly conjoined, and in a few hours Wormwood was gone. The house made a killing, and the following year Worm was promoted to head oddsmaker, the youngest in the state.

He circled a small dot on the south side of the valley. "I was thinking Seven Bridges," he said.

The Captain squinted at the map. "The hell's that?"

"Bottom of the valley. Nowhere settlement, tents and trailers. Maybe two, two-fifty."

"Huh. Where's the nearest bird?"

"About fifty miles upland," Worm said. "There's some prison crews working its east wing, but that's spit in the ocean."

"And who's your eyes out there?"

"Tower 18."

The Captain ran his finger along Worm's implied flight path. "Ruby, huh? Better watch out, the marks might accuse you of self-dealing, say the boy and his sister got themselves a scheme of some sort."

"You want I pick somewhere else?" Worm asked.

The Captain chuckled. "Christ, no. Personally, I don't see how it pays for us, but I know better than to doubt you. Go on, put it up on the board. Let's live a little."

Later in the morning the bookies and the accountant arrived, and at noon the betting house doors opened and the bouncers began to let the marks shuffle in. They were almost all men, tired drunks and seawall hands and salvage crew contractors and, although it was technically prohibited to take bets from anyone who did such work, hire-by-the-day firefighters. They placed bets with crumpled tens and twenties and spent as much or more money waiting on the burn reports in the Captain's bar across the street. They were men of slow ritual, mean-seeming but weak, and at the end of the day the losers among them could be seen tearing up and stamping their useless betting slips, their faces forest-red from the drinking and the small-making knowledge not that they had lost the previous day's wage but that likely they would lose the next one's too.

Most days, the man at the front of the line, sweltering under his union cap, was a ditch-digger named Miles. In the betting house they knew him as a tiresome four-settlement drunk, and but for his family ties to the house he would have been banned long ago, not for any single transgression, but for simply being more trouble than his ten-dollar bets made him worth.

The sound of the house doors opening woke Miles from his nap. He startled and eased himself slowly off the ground, patted the dead leaves off his pants. "About goddamn time," he said.

The men wandered in. The front of house, a wide space funnelling in toward the betting kiosks, was decorated along the walls with framed pictures of winners from years past, men who'd placed exceedingly ill-advised or ignorant bets that somehow paid off, and interspersed among these were other photographs of the valley and the forest as it had looked in prior seasons, and of other beautiful places—tropical islands and light-dipped waterfalls and the Hollywood

OMAR EL AKKAD

sign glimmering under rain—all of them far away in either distance or time. From the ceiling a discreet vaporizer filled the hall with the scent of cedar.

On the big board the men saw the pick of the day. Some said they knew the place and others pretended to know it and all loudly exchanged opinions and consulted their own sources of information, checking the notes they'd scribbled on their palms from whatever fire reports they read or heard about second-hand. All agreed that the pick was a lousy one, though the men were split on why. Eventually, opinion coalesced: there was no chance any bird could possibly reach Seven Bridges by midnight, and the men, buoyed by this invented communal certainty, began in droves to take the under.

Worm paced the back office. He called in again to Tower 18 and then 19 and 21 but there was no reply. Likely the smoke had killed the satellite reception, or perhaps all the watchers had retreated up out of the valley or simply left their posts for awhile; it was still early in the day and often the watchers timed their breaks for just after the betting houses put up their picks.

He heard a loud knocking on the backroom door. "Open up, goddammit," said the voice on the other side.

"Like clockwork." The Captain sighed. He turned to Worm, who shrugged.

The Captain motioned to one of the bookies, who unlocked the door. For a second the sound of the marks arguing in the betting hall became much louder, and then Miles walked into the back office and closed the door behind him. He pointed at Worm.

"What kind of loser line is that, Bryce?" he yelled. "You picking them out of a hat these days?"

"Old man, don't start," the Captain said.

"First of all, there ain't no bird within two days' flight of that dump, let alone one. Second, how you gonna let a boy pick a place one of his own got eyes on? What kind of ship you running here, Cap?"

96

Worm ignored both men. Again he tried the towers and again there was only static. Although it was frowned upon, he called a friend who worked another betting house's tower nearby, then a prison guard who ran convict brushclearing patrols on the side in that corner of the valley, but neither picked up. He stared at the wall map, its many intersecting lines, its many realities colliding.

"Hey, boy, I asked you a question?" Miles said.

Worm shook his head. "What?"

"I said, you trying to put this place out of business?"

"Go on back to the hall, Miles," Worm said. "Go across the street, have a drink. Better yet, go home, have a shower."

"Don't talk to me like that, boy. Don't nobody who picks a born loser tell me what to do."

"Christ, would you quit complaining," the Captain said. "If it's such a born loser, you take the under, you make some money. What's the problem?"

"I didn't take the goddamn under," Miles said. "I took the over." He flashed the house's little blue betting slip in Worm's direction. "You see that, boy? I took the over."

Miles walked back out into the betting hall, slamming the door behind him. It astounded Worm, how much the years hung on the old man. It wasn't so much the burns on his hands from working the sunfarm panels or the way all those years out in the forest with the shovellers had put a curve in his spine. It was just the wear of living. He remembered him younger, fuller somehow, in the years before he'd abandoned them, before Daughter Paradise burned, though those memories were shards now.

One of the bookies stood up and locked the door. "Twenty-one years that man been coming here," he said. "Twenty-one years. Could have bought a house up in cold country with the money he pissed away."

"He's Paradise born," the Captain said. "Stubborn people up there."

"That a granddaughter town?" the bookie asked.

"Great-granddaughter now. Burned up in '18, then again in '28 and '38. Every ten years, like they'd set a timer. They kept rebuilding in the same place, silly bastards. Got a museum there now with all the trinkets they salvaged each time, a bunch of teddy bears and wind chimes and vineyard signs. Some people got no sense at all."

The Captain shook his head. He looked at Worm then pointed at the cork board on the wall where the house kept the pictures and names of the permanently banned.

"Just say the word," the Captain said.

"You know I won't," Worm replied.

"Of course you won't. What kind of boy would?"

Word spread the betting house had picked a loser. In the hour before the book closed at three, a deluge of new marks had come in to take the under, and by close it was clear the house wouldn't be able to cover. Some of the marks began to complain, nervous now but excited; someone said they'd heard from a friend down south there wasn't so much as a black cloud in the sky over Seven Bridges. Eventually, after nightfall, as the men waited either for confirmation the town had burned or for midnight to roll round, Miles came knocking again on the back-office door.

"They're set to riot on you, Cap," he said. "Don't think you'll pay."

"When have I ever not paid, Miles?"

Miles shrugged. "I'm just the messenger, friend."

"Those suckers out there know you speak for them now?" The Captain chuckled. "The one genius who took the over on a sure dud?"

Miles smacked the side of the Remington safe. "Just better be ready to empty this thing, is all I'm saying."

"I tell you what, Miles," the Captain said. "I'll give you a mulligan, for old times' sake. I'll let you switch the bet, take the under at a half to one. How's that for a Christmas gift?"

"Shove it up your ass," Miles said. "I bought what I bought."

"Shut up," Worm said to the room, as another burst of static came through the handheld radio. "Ruby? You there?"

"It's a hell of a thing, Bryce," the voice on the other end said, low against the crackle and hum that every man in the room who'd been caught out by a bird before knew from memory. "Came up from the south. The whole time I was watching upland and then it came up from the south."

"Listen," Worm said. "Go down, get to the next tower over. Get to the river—"

"I swear it's a language," Ruby said. "A language all its own."

The radio cut. For a moment the back room of the betting house was silent. Worm felt the tightness coming on. He reached into a drawer and pulled out his inhaler, pried his lungs open.

"I'm going down there," he said.

"Going down where?" the Captain said. "You gonna drive a hundred miles south through logging roads and ash tracks? Then what, reason with it? Sit down."

The Captain picked up the phone and dialed a number Worm recognized as that of another betting house two counties over. "Put Garrison on," he yelled into the receiver.

"Garrison, I need you to call your tower boy out near 20-block, get me a read on some hole called Seven Bridges ... Don't give me that bullshit, Garrison ... Fine, 1 percent of the take ... 3 percent, that's it, take it or I swear we're done ... Good, call me back."

The men waited an hour, during which Worm tried calling every ranger station and watchtower within a hundred miles of Tower 18. Quickly it became clear the calling was futile, though no one in the back office would say this, or anything else, to Worm as he tried frequency after frequency, number after number.

At half past eleven the marks began banging on the door. Finally, the Captain let them in.

"The hell's going on, Cap?" one of the marks said. "We're a half hour from the bell and you got no updates for us? What kind of business you running here?"

The Captain came to respond but was interrupted by the office phone. A few of the marks inched their way into the back room to listen but the conversation was short and the Captain said only, "Yes, all right, thanks." He set the receiver down.

"Tower boy says a new one rolled up from south of the state border, out past our jurisdiction," he said. "He just got eyes on Seven Bridges now. Says it's gone."

The marks said nothing, confused but unwilling to admit it, then Miles spoke.

"Ain't no rule says where a bird's got to come from," he said.

"That's right," the Captain replied. He turned to the bookie. "The over pays on Seven Bridges," he said.

On hearing this, the marks groaned and shouted their disapproval. Some tore up their tickets and others said to keep them until the factfinders came back with real proof, and for a while Miles said nothing at all but then he started laughing, laughing and waving his little blue ticket in the air.

"A winner, a winner!" he said. "Goddamn, a winner!"

Quicker than the old man could react, Worm leaped from his seat and grabbed Miles by the collar of his shirt. A couple of bookies and marks stepped in to break the two men up but not before Worm had punched Miles in the face, a tooth and blood spittle coming out the man's slack mouth as his knees gave out beneath him.

"You did this," Worm said. "You did this."

"Did what?" Miles replied, grabbing his bloodied jaw and searching frantically for the winning ticket he'd dropped. "The hell did I do?"

A couple of marks stepped in to pull Worm away. "The hell's wrong with you?" one of them said. "What kind of a boy does a thing like that?"

Worm shoved the men aside. He stepped over Miles, dizzied, still on the ground, and left the back room. Out by the road he scanned frantically for logging trucks, convict crew vans, any vehicle that might be headed south, though he knew that even if such a vehicle were to come along, it'd be hours before he got anywhere near Seven Bridges, anywhere near Tower 18. Still, he ran up the road, helpless as a child, as behind him the marks began to spill out of the betting house, one of them clutching a fistful of bills and shouting: A winner. Goddamn, a winner.

MOTHER

Jowita Bydlowska

It is the time between the end of the night and the beginning of
the morning, not an actual hour, just that feeling of one thing
spilling into the next. The radio is on and they're playing the
new song by Cardi B, the one everyone over forty has strong
feelings about. I wonder what the Uber driver is thinking. I
assume that English is not his first language, which is why he
doesn't turn off the song. Otherwise he would find this awkward, driving a strange woman to the airport for money while
another woman sings about cunnilingus.

Maybe I am old. I am old. I'm in my forties, which is old.

I think about Alex, about him waking up to the apartment
strewn all around him, piles of bags and boxes lined up against
walls. I was trying to pack as much as I could before leaving: a
hamster tearing up wood chips of life, sorting, bagging, books,
tank tops, sweaters, a spatula, pictures of old classmates, a
bag of crystals—the fuck?—a vase, a Himalayan salt lamp . . .
packy-a-packy-packup-pack and then there was Alex kissing
the back of my neck and telling me everything was going to be
fine, just leave it, leave it, leave it, let's lie down.

We did lie down, he put his hand around my neck but not
tightly enough to choke me as he slowly slid into me, it was

perfect, it grounded me, I fell asleep for fifteen minutes and then it was time to go.

The song ends and another one starts but I don't recognize the artist. It's a bouncy thing, something about doing rails with Daddy. You read that right and I heard it right. Maybe.

The airport is quiet and empty. No one flies anymore unless essential or unless you're an asshole. The announcements implore travellers to tell the truth about having COVID. If you have any symptoms, please fess up. I'm sure any minute someone's gonna drop down to their knees: All right, fine, I do, I do, I can't lie any longer.

The airport has to do what it has to do to give us all a sense of being taken care of.

Daddy what? Rail me, Daddy.

I'm flying not because it's essential but because I'm an asshole. I've agreed to go on a writers' retreat that didn't get cancelled. Western Canada is business as before. On the plane, we are given disinfecting wipes to clean our seats. We will not be served any meals, only water. The plane is too quiet. The usual low-grade hysterics of flying seem to have been eradicated. There are no babies on the plane. A couple next to me erupts in a quick whisper fight over headphones. The plane takes off. I close my eyes and keep them closed for the duration of the flight.

I try to think about Alex again. While I'm away, he will move my stuff to our new apartment. I haven't told him that I am still not sure about this living together. He seems a lot more optimistic about it. He loves me. He tells me all the time.

At the airport, a man pulls my suitcase off the carousel. He doesn't realize his mistake and starts walking away with it. I yell after him but he can't hear me, AirPods jammed into his ears, so I end up running after him and tapping him on the shoulder. He looks me up and down like this is a club and I'm eyeing him.

Rail me, Daddy. I cover my mouth to stifle the giggle. It's the lack of sleep.

I point to my suitcase, he takes out his AirPods. I point to the little red string on the handle of the suitcase.

Oh shit, I'm so sorry, he says. His voice is deep and it reverberates somewhere in the middle of my chest. Oh shit, I think.

I don't know why I decide to wait with him for his suitcase but he says nothing when I turn around, he waits a beat, actually, as if we've agreed to walk back together so I walk back with him and by the time his suitcase arrives, I know his name is Yves and he's also going to the writers' retreat. What are the chances.

Yves takes his mask off after a few minutes of conversation, as if the virus is no longer a threat now that we've exchanged names and made suitcase blunders, but I guess since we're going to the same retreat, it is inevitable that we will at some point talk without our masks. There will be drinking. There always is at these retreats. And I can't imagine getting drunk with a group of masked strangers. We are sloppy. People are sloppy people.

We are to be picked up by the woman who organized the retreat, Susan Stone. Most published writers are only too happy to be invited to things. We are like lesser rock stars. Broke and demanding. But Susan loves people and she's an organizer. She says it's not true that talent is what separates a real writer from an aspiring one. She says the only difference between an unpublished writer and a published one is luck, which is not bullshit when I think about my own career. I guess I have had the luck. I have no idea how people decided that my writing had any merit. This conversation about luck and talent happens on the way to the retreat in the small town of Roseland.

Susan writes books about troubled young women losing memory and running away from serial killers. Lots of her characters get mutilated.

Susan is petite, blond, and partial to pinks and whites; she reminds me of a small butterfly and a piglet at the same time.

She speaks with a slight lisp. I've known Susan for years; we've been to the same authors' festivals and we share an agent. We are friends but not the kind of friends who talk often, just a once-in-a-while check-in and gossip about the boring industry we're part of. We have both slept with a tortured middle-aged Irish novelist many other young female writers have slept with. That's how we connected years ago when she found my texts on his phone. Neither of us was married to the novelist who was very much married to a woman in New York who owned a yoga studio. Susan said it was pointless to get mad at the novelist over his philandering; he wasn't her problem. Since I also had no feelings for him and I'm not a territorial kind of a person, I was happy to exchange medio-cre sex for a new female friendship. The novelist was exposed for his philandering and also for pretending to be somebody he wasn't; it was all over the news and I'm sure you've never heard of it because that's not your world's gossip, unless it is, in which case you know exactly who I'm talking about.

Susan asks Yves about Yves. Yves is from Quebec. He's published two books of poetry and a book of essays about art and love. I've seen his name before but never read him. He is tall and has a COVID beard, handsome guy, could be an extra from that TV show about Mexican drug lords. He's read what I've written or at least heard about it; everybody has read my short story collection in which I wrote about encounters like this one, in airports or at parties or in playgrounds where grownups meet to fulfill familial obligations and stave off sui-cide by suburbia. I wrote about hating parenting. I wrote about terrible men and terrible women who were terrible to each other. I've lived some of those stories, but most were made up.

I don't know why my stories became popular, but they did, maybe because a powerful mommy group picked up the collection for their book club and told other mommies. A famous actress bought film rights. There were some essays written about it, it was excerpted in *Elle* and *Hers*, and I went on breakfast television to talk about people hating parenting. And the big reveal was I wasn't even a parent! But I got it right. What I got right, I don't know, the boyfriend at the time said it was zeitgeist. He was also a writer but he claimed he's never been able to tap into the zeitgeist. He made it sound like dumb luck, which it was, again, everything is dumb luck unless you work hard or enter another dimension via spiritual awakening or psychosis. I make no sense. That's because I'm tired, it is late, and now I am in my hotel room alone, thinking about Yves.

Yves is married and has a baby at home, a toddler, and his wife is pregnant. Yves is on my floor of the small hotel, same floor as the hot tub, which is where we'll end up if not tonight then probably tomorrow after the welcome drinks. There will be other people with us but we will linger and we'll go out onto the terrace to have another glass of wine, then we'll be back in the tub and then this will go the way those things go in my stories and in real life. Which is, who knows.

I have no intention of cheating on Alex but I also didn't say I wouldn't. I know he feels insecure about the retreat, he's made jokes about me banging other writers and he's not wrong in how he perceives those things.

I don't quite get why Yves picked me. I mean, I knew at the airport—sometimes you know right away—but tonight we were introduced to a small cluster of aspiring young first-time novelists, a gaggle of breasts, yoga pants, and vegan flat shoes. The numbers are smaller than they normally are at these things, and there's no band and some of us are wearing masks so it's a little strange but we're all giggling about it, saying the same old thing about *post-apocalyptic* and *weird* and *back to normal.* I get the usual four ladies who want to tell me about their shitty husbands, one shy girl who wants to tell me about her mother, the worst relationship of her life.

Why? I say.

She says, Never mind.

Anyway, at some point the crowd gets smaller, and an aspiring writer from the Maritimes with a pink tie and hair like a small orange cloud tries to organize everyone; he's screaming something about the best seafood joint in town, and everyone leaves except for those of us who stay, in the lounge, and then the two of us in the tub.

It's hard with a baby, Yves says, and then he says other predictable things, things I write about that men say before they do something they don't really regret because they've been thinking about doing it all along. I don't ask him why he picked me, we both know this is just temporary and we're bored and attracted to each other. Sleeping with a fan girl would be a bad idea—she would write about it on her blog. I'm too old for that. I'm authentic. I authentically give off the vibe of wanting to be laid, I suppose, with my nonthreatening squeaky laughter and self-deprecating lines, and how I'm a little tired. Tired-looking and just tired, like I can't afford any more bullshit. I don't worry about wrinkling my forehead at the wrong moment. Some guys like that, younger guys like that.

In the hot tub, Yves slides up closer and I can smell him now and he smells fresh like he just shampooed his hair. We kiss. We are interrupted by the commotion at the door. A small group of drunks walks into the room and tumbles and plops themselves inside the hot tub and we're scrambling out despite their enthusiastic calls to please, please, the party is just starting, stay, stay, stay,

Sorry, sorry, sorry, we say, and leave. The carpet fibres feel sharp and unpleasantly plastic against my naked feet; my dress is clinging to my wet bikini. But it's warm and I don't shiver even though my body tries on a shiver that disappears instantly, unconvinced.

In his hotel room Yves shows me a sketchbook. This is a diversion from the script; in my stories it is always the woman's room, the man always leaves. Yves shows his drawings, like he needs to dazzle me extra, like being predictable unfaithful spouses at a retreat is not enough to have a tryst. But I look, I am interested, genuinely interested because I love boys who know how to draw. In school, those were the boys I was friends with, we all sat in the back of the classroom, me and those artsy boys. I was artsy too. I loved being able to compete with them, loved being able to make something as well as a boy could.

Yves's sketches are nice, mostly of people, up close a mess of cross-hatch lines and black ink absent spaces that when looked at from a distance make the blurry features stand out, give three-dimensionality to non-existent noses and make the eyes without the whites look right into you. Their blurry mouths move as if they were caught mid-talking. I love that detail.

I'm really good at reading lips, he says.

As I flip through the sketchbook, he kisses my neck and starts to undress me, one thin strap of my dress off my shoulder, the silk like a wave sliding down my side. I wear silk because I like its suggestion of sleep, of sex; this summer women's shops are full of sleepwear, appropriately, as the world goes in and out of lockdown and we live in our beds for days as the government mandates our collective depression.

I miss my mother. I don't talk to my mother anymore and I miss her. She is probably alone and she has no idea where I am. I hope she is at home, her cats like fluffy pillows around her bald head, naked shoulders. The image makes me gasp and the whole thought about her explodes inside me, and muffles the little almost-sounds of silk and sucking and licking and whatever's happening.

I wish I could tell Yves why I suddenly stiffen under his touch, why I shake my head when his hand snakes up my thigh, why the sketchbook falls out of my hands. He is asking what is wrong and then he says that he agrees with me that this is wrong, and what is wrong with him and he should call his wife, this was a mistake—he says all those things that you'd imagine a man in his situation saying as he tries to straighten out, as he lifts the straps of my dress and pulls my dress back over my breasts, the waves of silk rippling and then settling back on my body.

I am saying things too, I am apologizing, I am telling him it's not him, and it's not me either—I try to make that joke but it falls flat. I say that it's my mother, despite myself I am telling him the real reason why even though I know it will only make everything more confusing. We will have to go through this week sitting awkwardly in shared spaces and awkwardly making small talk when alone, and there will be all those looks, unanswered beginnings of sentences, and uhsaehmshmms because nothing, almost nothing happened. And it's worse to have nothing happen in the space of where it was supposed to be happening. It's worse to have almost nothing rather than *something* you could feel guilty or excited or confused about. Thank god for this sketchbook, I think, at least that will be a thing we can talk about—art, drawing, and how come he didn't pursue it, or something along those lines. I will probably find out he has an Instagram where he posts his drawings, not too many followers, because it's nothing special, it's just a thing he does, seriously.

Before all of that, and now, here in this space with my revelation of "mother" we are sitting beside each other on the edge of his bed.

My mother is sick, I add.

Your mind is preoccupied, he says.

I nod because that's exactly it.

I'm sorry. I understand. My mother died when—

My mother is not dying, I say, but I am not sure if that's true because like I said, I no longer talk to her. My sister emailed me in the morning saying I should probably get in touch but that she won't be a *conduit* anymore, an odd choice of a word.

I've always wondered if I was stupid. How would I know? This is not a self-esteem issue; this is a serious concern I have. It is

also a question my mother used to ask me; she is not someone whose presence enhanced my life. But it's pedestrian to
hate one's mother, and it is perhaps stupid. This is the real
reason I wonder if I am stupid—because I cannot get over
my resentment. It stops me in my tracks. And I don't mean
figuratively—I can be walking somewhere and a memory will
pop into my head—my mother's wild red curls shaking as
she screams about one thing or another—and I will stop, my
breath suddenly a choke. In the middle of a sidewalk, on an
escalator. I have to let it play till the end. It's my own YouTube
of trauma, no ads, no break.

I asked a therapist once: Am I incurable? She said as long as
there was somebody else in my life who loved me, who showed
me real love I would be all right. Even a teacher, a friend, somebody else's mother. One person only and I could reverse the
damage, erase the words or at least mute them, prove them to
be the wrong words said about me. The therapist didn't ask me
if there ever was somebody like that, she probably assumed
there was because I remember smiling and nodding and her
nodding back and smiling encouragingly as if I did in fact
name a person like that.

I didn't go to therapy because of my mother, it was something else. Not changing clothes for a couple of days in a row;
limp, greasy hair, somebody noticed, a supervisor in my dorm.
Off to talk to a professional. We talked about my mother but
only because you talk about mothers in therapy.

I didn't go for a long time and I suddenly felt lighter. One
day I woke up and my energy was back and I was no longer
gasping for breath from unidentified grief or whatever it was
that put me in bed. I can't even remember what the therapist
looked like, I just remember those little moments, the smiling
and nodding and how the couch felt, too worn-out and soft,
the brownness of it all. And I remember not being able to
come up with my antidote person. There were always men
who tried to rescue me, even back then in my undergrad.

There was a boy who moved with me from the small town where I grew up. He urged me to move out of my dorm and into the dingy apartment he sold weed out of. I packed a few garbage bags one day and paid some friends in pizza to help me start my new life as a live-in girlfriend. I didn't know if the boyfriend loved me unconditionally or enough to make up for my mother's abuse but soon I forgot about my criteria and focused on the nice aspect of sharing space with a male, which meant sex. I could get lost in sex, I had easy orgasms and I was happy with my body even as it slowly grew larger, no longer scrutinized by dorm mates who watched obsessively what they and everybody else ate. I achieved a state of contentment, settling into a routine of sex, weed-smoking, and exquisite midnight grilled cheese sandwiches, the making of which was one of the few things my boyfriend learned from his own mother who loved him enough. I knew she loved him enough because she disliked me, she was suspicious of my going to university and she called me a snob. She was under the impression that it was my idea to live in a large city, and she resented that her son dropped out of school to follow me.

Eventually, she convinced the boyfriend to leave me and move back home.

I am thinking of all the other mothers I've met and know— dozens of mothers of friends and boyfriends and mothers of strangers on Facebook and even in movies and books. Not the hideous ones from the horror trope, just regular, imperfect mothers but also mothers who are almost perfect. Not the extremely perfect mothers who scheme and kill and sacrifice their own lives to push their babies through the membranes of life. But the behind-the-scenes mothers, the ones who are authentic and warm and a little embarrassing but who are keepers of secrets and defenders of faults, to whom the word *proud* tastes sweet and addictive so they have to say it over and over—*Mom, sto-op*—but they never stop so the pride is an invisible armour grown by their children who are baffled but nonplussed when someone who is not their mother is not proud. I'm talking about the mothers who talk to their daughters every night, the best-friend mothers, the sister-mothers, the mothers who bake and cook, and send care packages. The mothers who take on another job to pay for piano lessons, who form groups, who advocate and start foundations and marches, or participate in foundations and marches—not to be seen as Great Mothers but because it's the right thing to do. I'm talking about mothers who have met their daughters' best friends, mothers who are friends with the best friends, mothers who were phoned the morning after their daughters happily lost their virginity.

Mothers who never said, I don't know who's going to drive you to the abortion clinic but not me, when in a moment of joyous oblivion the daughter let her usual guard down and made such phone call the morning after.

Who would I even have called had I had to find my way to the abortion clinic? It was a good thing I smartened up right away that morning. I called a friend's mother—of course—and she drove with me to a gynecologist who put me on birth control. The mother didn't understand why I was crying but I couldn't tell her, I couldn't take the humiliation of having to rely on a strange mother for mothering.

I call Alex from the writers' retreat and he says that everything went well, I am all moved in, and all I need to do is just relax and enjoy myself and come back to him when I'm ready. That's a joke, it's not like I've run away so I'll be back when I'm supposed to be back. He's set up the bedroom and bathroom but he doesn't know where all the kitchen stuff goes but he's making some lasagna and a bean salad, would I like anything else? He's bought some mango kombucha, a whole litre of it and I won't even believe the organic store he's found in our new neighbourhood.

I am touched, I feel tender. I want to tell someone but I don't know who I can share my Alex story with; I am not one of those women who gushes about her new boyfriend to anyone who would listen and I haven't gotten close with anybody on the retreat except for Yves who I manage to avoid. There are twelve other people in the hotel, people who have books they've been working on their entire lives, memoirs and novels about sea monsters, and detective series. It is thanks to those people that Yves, Sue Stone, and I attend the retreat for free. We are the writers who have been published, we are the promised guests. We spend our entire days reading manuscripts and going for walks with the Unpublished, the evenings are devoted to getting drunk and sharing stories about other writers' retreats and conferences with workshops on how to pitch novels. The Unpublished all have sent out their work to various agents, including New York ones. Two nights in a row, I retreat to bed early claiming a headache. I can feel Yves watching me but so what? Tonight, when I join everyone for dinner, Yves is sitting close to a young Chinese writer who is writing a memoir about cooking traditional dishes and how dumplings brought her closer to her culture because—

At dinner, still buzzing with feeling happy about Alex, I send a text to my sister to tell her that my move went smoothly. I don't ask about our mother. I don't know what to ask and how.

You should stay, Susan says when I get up to go. Her hand is firm on my forearm and I understand what she's saying. I am a monkey paid to perform. I cannot claim a headache again, I have to be here with these people and I have to give them their money's worth.

Let's get drunk, somebody suggests. Really drunk.

We all get really drunk. It is the usual. Drunk, elbow-holding instant friend conversations. My phone buzzes a few times. I pull it out of my pocket at one point but Susan, again, is there to discipline and I put the phone away but not before noticing the seven notifications from my sister.

My mother is dead.

I don't know how I know it but I do.

Somebody tells a joke and I laugh too hard. I want to draw attention to myself. Yves's attention. He's still with the young Chinese writer but he's looking at me as I laugh and I don't look away.

I'm so messed up, I mouth and he nods. He mouths something back but I am not good at reading lips like he is. I walk toward him, and the room is swaying. Somebody walks up to me and says she's thinking of leaving her husband.

Great, I say, and she looks at me with big, hurt eyes.

I'm sorry, I say but I hate her right now, hate her and her intrusion, hate that she's stopping me as I'm on my way to make this a lot worse.

I see Susan looking at me and Yves as we leave the room and I see the Chinese writer looking too. I don't care. I'm feeling aggressive and sexy. I remember the Cardi B song about cunnilingus. I want to listen to it right away and I pull out my phone but then remember the texts and shove it right back into my pocket. It's strange that alcohol hasn't given me the courage to read what it says. I'm on a different mission now.

We end up in my room. It's how it is in my stories. He kisses me, he cups me between my legs, he peels off my silk dress. He puts his hand around my neck—I guess everyone watches the same porn now. I enjoy the feeling of his taut skin against mine, so different from Alex who is a little plump and my age. I don't have a thing for young guys. But I do as my characters do, I go along with the script.

He comes on my stomach. I don't come at all. I consider asking if he's got anything—chlamydia, syphilis—but the question—at this point in this story—strikes me as so stupid, I burst out laughing. I feel nauseous.

My mother was healthy her entire life. She didn't deserve this health. She had terrible habits—smoking, drinking, yelling.

But her body didn't care and kept going. She came to visit me in my old apartment and she told me I was a failure. At my age, living alone, with no family, in a place like that. That's not how she raised me. I wasn't sure how she raised me. That was just a fight like every other fight we had but for some reason I decided I would no longer attempt to forgive or make up. I would have to learn how not to care. When she turned sixty-five, she fell ill. I didn't know what was wrong. I talked to my sister and she said cancer. Of course it was cancer, a banal serial killer that lays waste to women more than men do. My sister said it was bad, she had ascites, a fluid buildup in the abdomen, which is always a bad sign; it meant that her disease was advanced. This was when the pandemic was just starting, a few weeks before the entire country, then the world went into the lockdown. My sister went to treatments and she said our mother was impatient with doctors, but didn't fight them, she just let them administer needles and pills and the only wish she had was a subscription to all the movie channels. All of them. She was always frugal, never even got cable and had an old laptop that she referred to as "my computer machine."

I remember that now, that little phrase, *my computer machine*.

I am in my hotel room, my packed suitcase on my bed, a signed book of poetry from Yves on top of it. He wrote, *Thank you for everything*.

Everything what? In bed, earlier, he said our meeting was like a door opening. To what? He said I made him feel alive.

A new baby will also make you feel alive, I joked, and he glared at me.

I suppose, he said. He was getting dressed, he struggled with one sock, it seemed narrower than the other one. I wondered if it was perhaps his wife's sock; it was a black sock, an easy mistake.

We were going to the airport in an hour. Everyone ran around the hotel, exchanging numbers and last-minute confessions and tips about how not to get published. You need luck, there is no tip to be given about that. So whatever they were saying to each other—wait at least eight weeks before writing to enquire about your novel, again, read their book lists—was useless. In that past week, during afternoon readings, I heard some good writing, I thought how it was relatively subjective, this process of choosing who should see their shit in print, really. Nobody was bad, they all had talent. Even the ones who wrote about werewolves. In my head, I wished them all luck. I could tell bad writing because I once taught a group of women at a community centre; it was a class on writing personal stories, short memoirs. That experience taught me that some people should never write. I didn't know what to do with sentences lacking a subject, verb, and predicate. I didn't wish those women luck, I wished them to be able to find other hobbies. But out loud, I did say, Good luck!

Yves sits beside me on the plane. His hand is under the blanket, I squirm against his arm, inhale his sweater, which smells of lavender. I wonder if he has moths at home.

The plane is quiet as before, we keep wiping our seats and headphones, and no one talks. No babies again.

When the plane touches the ground, I pull out my phone. There are twelve texts. All from my sister.

Our mother opted for assisted suicide. My sister texts there is a letter for me. *Our mother was very brave. You know how pragmatic she is. She doesn't want to be a burden.* She hated having to go for treatments all alone. Relatives were not allowed because of the lockdown restrictions and it was just too much for her, to have to sit in the chemo chair all on her own, with poison pumping into her veins. There was no point, she was stage 4, why prolong it?

My sister writes she is not prepared to talk about what it was like to sit with our mother during her last moments. *Funniest thing, she did the dishes and swiped the floor before like she had a to-do list or something.*

Funniest thing that's not funny. Unfunniest. And she probably did have a to-do list.

I don't know what to write back to my sister. *Sorry?* I type the word just to see how it would look in response to her text, and it is as ridiculous as the shit emoji. I find a face that has no mouth, just eyes. That's what I send her as a response to everything that she's written. That's the kind of person I am. A speechless kind of person.

In her last text, my sister writes that she isn't mad at me because what I've done to myself is enough punishment. She is right.

Yves and I don't exchange phone numbers or any other coordinates. I mean, social media, you don't need to do that kind of thing to get in touch but not exchanging numbers is an agreement that we will not get in touch. I say to him, I hope the baby is healthy and I wish you all the happiness.

I'm going to write a poem about you.

Please don't.

I take a taxi to my new address and the same Cardi B song comes on, how funny, but the words are all bleeped out so it's just one long hiccup with some beats that goes on for three minutes. Outside the windows, the city is the same slog of incompetence in the shape of steel and glass. A giant blown-up gorilla bounces in the air above a car dealership. If you were a first-time visitor nobody would blame you for asking to turn around and drive back to the airport.

My new neighbourhood is a hangover with some vomit splattered on its shirt. Shufflers everywhere and dads without scarves dragging their *filthy, sturdy unkillable infants** through dug-up sidewalks. Dogs in strollers.

The taxi stops, I get out and inhale the wretchedness.

---

* Ezra Pound, The Garden

I comfort myself with my usual anxiety-appeasing thought: 90 x 0.5 mg, 60 x 1 mg, vodka, hop. Clonazepam, zopiclone hoarded, and then the bridge. I have access to all four. I'm not as brave as my mother but it brings me comfort to know that I have the option. I don't have the option because I don't have the desperation. My mother really was the bravest, and I am sorry I didn't know. I miss her more than ever, now. What would I do with that hole? Should I pin a flower right in the centre of my chest to stop the bleeding, stop the guilt; staple a rose to my breast—good enough?

My building is called Everglades. Beige brick, a door dark red like a blood clot. A tiny woman in a coat as big as a sleeping bag, wide-eyed above the blue surgical mask, opens the door and stares at me, her eyes narrowing as I come closer.

Where do you live? she screams in a voice that's equally threatening and scared.

Here, now, I say.

She groans what sounds like a swear word, she shakes her head, jumps away from me as if tasered and scuttles off.

Alex is home. He pulls me into a hug and holds me for a long time as I sob. Without evidence, I know he can smell Yves in my DNA, he can smell whatever is still smouldering from the witch's burning stake. He says nothing. That's what I most like about him, what has made me fall in love with him, actually, him not saying anything when there are no words to describe what could possibly be said. And I remember: *All you need is just one who truly loves you.*

My mother is dead, I finally speak, and he sighs. It's the kind of a sigh that pulls you in; it's a depth of a sound, a filter through darkness, bottom of a murky lake, an underwater camera, lens on top of a lens switching rapidly to make a blurry image clearer, bass, and softness, and sonorousness, and tenor, and static.

YOUR HANDS ARE BLESSED

(or *Yis Lemli Hidayki* in Arabic)

Christine Estima

When Cousin Emil's wife, Marwan, disappeared on her way home from the university, Sito was finally persuaded to leave Damascus. The refugee camp was just over the border in Lebanon. It was already full of Syrians, but Sito recognized no friends or neighbours. There were families from Homs and Aleppo, and the more industrious ones were selling food and water. Their white tents became shops decked in sheet metal and tin. Bottles of water for one lira. The flatbreads were made with black flour, and the loaves were made with too much yeast so they would rise quickly. The soups, comprised of boiled barley and beans, were made with unclean water. The meat was just fermenting salami and probably goat or desert hog.

Sito had been a piano teacher all her life; what did she know of selling wares? Emil tried to show her how she might be useful. He got his hands on long needles and thin Bemberg fabric, but after years of being a concert pianist, her knuckles and joints hurt. It was a dull ache deep inside as if she slept on her hands the wrong way.

"*Baladi, baladi ...*" she would repeat when she thought no one could hear her. *My country, my country ...*

Sito and Emil were in the refugee camp for eight months before I was able to bring them to Montreal. Sponsoring them privately meant that I had to demonstrate I could cover the cost for a year so I took out a second line of credit. They flew into the international airport in Toronto. My six-hour drive there flew by quickly like migrating magpies. They came out of the arrival hall wearing new winter jackets. A few months earlier, a big hullaballoo had been made by our prime minister personally handing out parkas, smiling with his hand over his heart. Now, there were no cameras. The airport was white with green carpeting.

Emil was pushing the valise cart, and Sito gripped his arm. She looked like a half-mast flag in the wind.

I greeted them with kisses and hugs. I was so glad to have my Sito again. She used to hold me when I was young and feed me bits of kibbeh ("because it's good for you") in between bites of *bit'leywa* ("don't tell your mother"). She used to feed the birds on her back balcony, the scent from the cedar trees wafting through the air. The building's courtyard echoed the false notes of her piano students. I grew to hate Beethoven's Seventh or Chopin's Nocturne in F Minor, but for some reason, not even the sloppiest student could sully Erik Satie.

"*Ib khibic, Sito!*" *I love you.*

"*Ana ib khibic camaney ...*" she meekly replied. *I love you too.*

"*Siti inti helwa! Inti chatra!*" *My Sito is so sweet and smart.*

"Oh knock it off," she mumbled as we loaded into the car. She refused my hand when offered; her eyes black like a starling.

We rode back to Montreal on a sun-dappled day, and everything seemed to have so much promise. I pointed out the large Canadian flag in Joyceville, the Big Apple in Colborne, and we stopped at the Dairy Queen in Lancaster so she could have a taste of cold.

We crossed the border into Quebec and the cracked asphalt, peppered with potholes, made Sito's headscarf topple to her shoulders. She never pulled it back up.

Emil wasted no time in getting a job unloading crates at the Marché Jean-Talon, so he was out the door every morning by 4:00 a.m., bless him. With just the two of us remaining, I'd sit on our front porch with Sito during the quiet stillness of morning. She wanted her coffee black and to feed the birds. She'd never seen squirrels before, outside of American movies, and they ate all the feed and chased the swallows away. This made her laugh. She didn't understand the Montreal ritual of walking with your coffee. "Why don't they sit and drink it? Why is everyone showing off their coffee to the neighbourhood?"

"They've got to go to work, Sito. It's coffee on the go."

On the go was not something she'd ever heard of.

From the porch, every Thursday morning before garbage collection, we would watch the Chinese ladies with their shopping carts go from bin to bin, pulling out bottles and empties. Sito watched them with a hawk's eye. She didn't ask questions, even though she asked questions about everything—why are all the stairways on the outside of the houses here? Why do we have so many bagels in the fridge? Why do you eat maple syrup on snow? What is a tam-tam? Why do you swear on Catholic chalices and not Orthodox ones? Who is this Simonaque you keep mentioning?

But with the Chinese ladies, she was silent, cataloguing every nuance and detail. They dragged their wine carts behind them or pushed their shopping trollies. They wore rubber gloves and had many reusable shopping bags. They opened each blue recycling bin and then whipped out a small flashlight no bigger than a finger. They'd tilt the bin one way, look

123

inside, pull out the malachite bottles and brightly coloured empties, tilt the bin the other way, and again flash the light. Then one more tilt for good measure. Up and down the streets they went, putting all they found in their carts until they were full. One lady hung bags off her bicycle handles. One woman used a rolling dolly. They came dressed for tempests, gales, and snowstorms.

Sito watched as our neighbours ran out to give them their bottles with a quick hello and smile. She noticed people across the street leave their empties next to the bins on purpose so the ladies didn't have to dig.

The ladies had their turf too. West of Saint-Urbain was this lady's, east of Saint-Laurent was that lady's. No going north of Van Horne for this lady, no going south of Laurier for the other. Mile End evenly divided.

Our side of the street belonged to June. I didn't know much about June. Her French wasn't great but she could make herself understood. If I'm being honest, I liked June. She didn't bother me with chit-chat, and she didn't rattle my bins as loudly as the other ladies. She was to-the-point and I salute that kind of dedication. Leaving her my empties was a pleasure. Sometimes I would find a pecan tart on my stoop with a note: *Merci! — de June.* Another time, six sparkling Christmas ornaments. Foaming hand soap that smelled like a vanilla candle. She did the same for my neighbours too. Alexandre next door got two new colouring books for his girls. Frederique on the corner got a Chinese Osmanthus flower cake.

Sito was oddly transfixed.

After a while, it got to be that Sito wanted to spend her mornings going for a walk, so she offered to get us coffees every day from the Haddad Sisters, a Lebanese bakery down the street. If everyone did a "coffee walk," she might as well do what the Montréalais do. And at least at the Haddad Sisters she could speak Arabic.

She did this every morning, so I left money on the credenza for her. She was always an early riser anyway, like five forty-five, so by the time I'd rise around seven fifteen, she'd be sitting at the dining room table with our coffees and some *sfi'ha* for us to nibble on.

One morning I was up at six fifteen. My thoughts were rolling around in my head, festering, and rotting. Things weren't great with Sullivan since Sito came. How was I supposed to see him? He couldn't come here now, and I could hardly sneak away to his place. He was frustrated but also understanding and gentle, which made things even worse. If he was an incomprehensible and unmitigated ass, a breakup would be easy. But no, he had to be sensible and kind. As I lolled out of bed and went to the dining room, Sito wasn't back from the Haddad Sisters. And she still wasn't back by six thirty. Or six forty-five.

"Did you get lost?" I asked her when she finally rolled in with a tray of coffee and *sfi'ha*. She had quietly locked the door behind her but jumped at the sound of my voice. Surprised to see me awake and standing in the corridor, she looked at me like she was fresh out of things to say. "No." She brushed past me to go sit at the dining room table.

Sullivan pulled me aside one day in the break room.

"No," I whispered. "I thought we agreed never to do this here."

"Don't worry, just a friendly hello from a work buddy." He smiled as he poured himself a coffee from the slow-drip and topped mine up. "Where's your head at these days?"

"I'm sorry, I know, I've really been absent."

Sullivan had this way of making me apologize without ever even expressing hurt. He sipped from his mug and kept his eyes on the warehouse floor just beyond the break room windows. The home and garden centre team were watering the strawberry plants and the plumbing and electrical experts were guiding DIYers to the nozzles and plugs aisle.

"I used to think at times I could read your mind," he said into the mug, our eyes never meeting. "But now, it's . . ."

"It's Sito," I said. "I think she's trying to pull a fast one."

"She's your grandmother, not a moody teen."

I snorted. "You don't know her. She's sneaking away every morning."

He put the mug down, wiped his hands on the back of his reflector vest, and reached for my hand. "Well, if she's stowing away, maybe you could too?" His hand was clammy and calloused.

Slipping out of his palm, I walked briskly back to the power tool section.

Waiting for Sito to come home each morning made me develop a strange relationship with my living room. I came to know each small crevice and crack, and watched them expand and contract with the passing hours. I washed the floors again and again, and stepped on them too soon in socks. I cried on the couch while my cat consoled me. I cooked too much oatmeal. Even ate it too. I formed an unbreakable bond with yogurt. I dreamed of dinner parties with dear friends, introducing them to Sito and Sullivan, and being comfortable in that. The ticking clock on the wall mocked me. *Who do you think you are?* it asked.

One afternoon on his day off, I sat with Emil as tears, like peach blossoms, fell from his eyes.

"I never loved anyone like I loved Marwan." His lower lip trembled and his chin collapsed. All this time, he had been holding out hope that she was just in another refugee camp. Maybe she was injured and lost her memory. Maybe she'd find her way back to Emil. A new life in Montreal was so close for them both. But after many inquiries with the UNHCR, that was looking less likely.

"Why did I let her walk alone?" he berated himself. "Why didn't I walk with her?"

"Knowing Marwan, she would have shooed you away," I said. "She was too proud for an escort."

Emil hung his head like a swaying ornament, but then started to nod. "I should have followed her."

I wanted to hold his hand but he balled it into a fist. I covered it with my palm as he watched the swallows migrating across the sky beyond the window. "I'd have all the answers to my questions if I just stayed a few metres behind her."

I sat at the wheel of my car, sitting on my cold hands, waiting for Sito to emerge. Having set my alarm and slipped out of the house unnoticed, I wanted to get a jump on her without alerting her. When she finally came out the front door, she paused on the porch to tie her headscarf under her chin like a kerchief. She hadn't worn a headscarf around me since the drive from Toronto, but now she slowly took the porch steps down to the sidewalk, and pulling a slim wine cart behind her, she walked up the street, her headscarf like armour. I put the car into gear.

When she passed the turn for the Haddad Sisters, and stopped on the sidewalk to chat briefly with June, I pulled the car over. She walked to the side of a house, opened up the recycling bin, tipped it this way and that, pulled out three cans and two green bottles, loaded her wine cart, and wiped her hands on the brim of the windbreaker I had given her.

I sat in my car for a long time, engine off, gripping the wheel until my knuckles were ivory-plated and the dry skin cracked. She disappeared up one side of the street, reappearing down the other. I called Sullivan but there was no answer.

She slipped down a side alleyway to the next street. Following her on foot, I saw her pop into the local SAQ. June and some of the other women were already there. Through the window, she disappeared to the rear of the shop behind the racks of Italian and French wine, headed for the bottle return.

When I got back to my car, Sullivan had texted. *Was sleeping.* The hot tears bloomed, brimmed, and fell like stones.

When Sito came home, I was sitting on the porch, waiting for her. Her headscarf was down about her shoulders.

"*Habibti*," she said to me like a question. "Look."

Reaching down into the wine cart that had a faint boozy stench, she pulled out a lemon sugar cake wrapped in cellophane. She held it like she was cupping a sparrow.

"Did you get that at the Haddad Sisters?" I asked.

She sat next to me and placed it on her lap. "Would you like a slice?"

Nodding to her, I rubbed my hands together; the only thing keeping me from talking more. The lemon cake was moist and still warm, with a hint of za'atar spice, cloves, and lemon zest. Crumbs fell into the ends of my hair.

The money I left her for coffee sat untouched on the credenza, and were I to question her further, she would have no choice but to tell me everything. *I know*, I could say, *what you're doing. If you needed extra money, why didn't you just ask me?*

But I didn't say anything. Because I couldn't.

We sat silently as the sky turned from a hazy salmon to bright linseed, eating our cake.

"Montreal is a fine city," Sito said after a while.

My hands folded in my lap, almost as if they were praying.

RIVER CROSSINGS
Carmelinda Scian

I stand at the mouth of the Tejo, the vast Atlantic lost beyond the dull horizon, the bustling city behind me. Car horns, guitars, drums, chatter, fill the air. It begins to drizzle. A sudden gust of wind ruffles the wide, restless river. Out of the mist, a chrysalis of grey river and overcast sky, a skinny girl, brown eyes open wide, emerges, mollusks on her hair. She beckons me, skeletal arm reaching, reaching…I see her tears. They meld with the raindrops, the river, the mist. I wipe my eyes. Gulls cry angrily above my head. Deafening. Disarming. Haunting.

For whom are they crying?

I have no umbrella. But I remain fixed on a drama only I can see.

A massive white screen has been erected next to the equestrian statue of King José I in the monumental square facing the river. This is where the king's residence used to be before the devastation of 1755. The statue celebrates the rebuilding of the city after the earthquake. This screen, too, must be a celebration. Then I remember: the 2018 World Cup. Portugal vs. Uruguay. Later today. Cristiano Ronaldo comes to mind. Our modern hero. Other names follow, those who navigated these waters long ago. Vasco da Gama, Álvares Cabral, Magalhães, who set out in discovery of sea routes, lands, spices, riches, power. Later, fishermen followed. They salted cod on the shores of Newfoundland. Their faces and names are not known, not remembered or recorded. But they opened the doors to future immigrants, men and women ready to confront the unknown. Begin anew. Ha, the new-found-land on the other side of these turbulent waters, where I have lived, trying to forget the very land I'm standing on. Yes, yes, trying to forget a childhood spilling over with brutality masqueraded as love from a mother whose insanity was never diagnosed. Never, it was never she who had a problem. Four decades spent at the smithy of life trying to cobble a new me.

Yet . . .

You stand on the upper deck of the old ferry crossing the Tejo from Montijo to Lisboa. The wide river is tempestuous on this grey November morning. The waters are angry. It'll take an hour to cross. You shiver, pull your green woollen scarf tighter around your neck. You look behind you. There's no one. *Good.* You want to be alone in this long-awaited farewell. This departure from everything you've known up to now. You glance back at Montijo. The bullring in the distance, the black mountains of garbage at the river's entrance, Lisbonites sending their refuse across on barges. In summer, stench and flies undo good intentions. The black mountains of garbage darken the sky, like monolithic guards at a Stygian passage to a subterranean kingdom. Behind Montijo lies Amendoeiro, where you lived, that ad hoc town of unpaved streets, whirling dust, stray cats and dogs, whores, drunkards, beggars, gossip, the lingering terror of Salazar's regime, the sweaty hands of your grandfather's greasy-haired tenant next door on those parts of your body that made you feel ashamed when you were only eight! You never told anyone. Left behind the swells vomited by the ferry too is the dread of your mother's anger, her beatings, the savagery of her exactitude—you were always deficient. But you're turning sixteen next month; soon you'll be too old to be beaten into submission. Behind too are the shameful piss-pots under the beds, the manure pile of shit and food leftovers at the back of the garden, and Eduardo, the buck-toothed idiot your mother chose as your boyfriend. He's in the ferry's bar at this moment drinking coffee with her, planning your future. Soon he'll be left standing at Lisbon Airport with you waving goodbye. Forever goodbye. You've imagined this scene a thousand times. In a few hours, your mother, Manuelito, and you, will be in a Canadian Pacific plane away to Toronto to join your father. A new larger world is waiting for you.

The Tejo girdles the ancient white city, whose foundation predates recorded history, eternally watching it. It begins to ebb, unveiling its black muddy bottom. There's something disarming, disappointing, forlorn in the nakedness of the river. Waves of dread run through me making me feel vulnerable. Afraid. I can't speak. Claudio fears my silence, he fears being left out of my world but he says nothing. Draws me close. The drizzle persists. We buy an umbrella from a Chinese vendor. She says *obigado* instead of *obrigado*.

We walk the old city, Alfama, Chiado, Bairro Alto, Belém, a maze of cobblestone streets with shops, restaurants, crowds, laughter, a hymn to the dark past—smashed bones and screams of terror in the night—and a cheer to this bustling EU present. Newcomers now fill the city for whom Portugal's past has no meaning. These changes dissolve the familiar, warping my earlier memories of Lisbon. Now people of different colours and ethnicities stand at establishment doors, calling us in. Indians hawk the traditional *pastéis de nata*; an Angolian sells us the port wine we'll take to my cousin Margarita tonight for a family dinner. A reunion of sorts. Lisbon's doors are open; the world descends on this native soil. A new aurora heralds from every corner.

Before dinner, my cousins ask me about my mother. They know that it's been years since we've spoken, know too that my first marriage, to Eduardo, was her idea. "Last week I called my parents," I say in Portuguese with a chuckle, meant to entertain, to amuse these relatives I haven't seen in years. They sit around me, forward, intense, wide-eyed, showing interest. "After four decades," I say, "I was sure my mother had forgiven me ..." I start to cry, softly at first, then sobs roll over me like a bulldozer, storming this safe space. Claudio comes closer.

"Stop," he says.

My cousins are all silent; I've frightened them. A fifty-year-old woman sobbing like a child isn't pretty.

Time morphs.

The rain pounding the windows of the CP plane seems wrathful, as though determined to destroy it. The Tejo below looks black, menacing. Cristo Rei, colossal, across the river, blesses the city and the river crossings, those departing or arriving, as destiny decrees. You pray Cristo Rei is blessing you.

Your mother sits behind you with Manuelito. You hear her sighs and wonder if the other passengers are also hearing her. Her promise to Eduardo, as they embraced, still rings loud in your ears. Both were crying like two broken-hearted lovers in some melodrama. "Don't worry," she said. "I'll call for you as soon as possible." You hurried past the gate.

In Montreal, two men in uniform ask you questions. You don't understand what they're saying; they don't seem to understand you. But you're not frightened. They smile, voices soft, blue-gazes welcoming, assuaging the strangeness, the disarming sense of dislocation running through you. They are different from the terrifying authoritativeness of Portuguese officials using the vocabulary of threat and intimidation.

You feel this new world is opening wide—*wide* ... It's calling you. *There, there ... You can almost touch it.*

RIVER CROSSINGS

You're told by a clerk speaking Portuguese that the flight from Montreal to Toronto is a short one. An hour. But the plane is small, claustrophobic, wobbling in the vacuum of the skies, as though trying to duck some unseen enemy. The pilot announces that there's a snowstorm. FASTEN YOUR SEAT-BELTS, the lit-up signs say.

Your mother now sits next to you; Manuelito is across the aisle. She's crying: "I'll never forgive your father."

It's late when the plane arrives. The airport feels ghostly. Your father is waiting with a man and a woman and a girl your age. You don't know them. The girl is dressed in a Cinderella-like long dress, blue lace and tulle, as though at a costume party. You have a strange feeling that you are travelling back in time, that the new world is receding into something unrecognizable.

A trial. It feels like a trial, this last supper. I'm surrounded by a jury of cousins sitting around the dinner table. It's behind their smiles, in their eyes. I catch them. Suspended knives and forks in mid-air when they least expect. They stare at me, wanting to know, figure things out, reach a verdict that will satisfy them because my mother was loved by them too. A favourite with her kindness and open-arm generosity. They want to make a choice. Decide which one of us is guilty. Then they can go forward with their lives, pick sides, stop the arguments.

But it's a tale not for the pure of heart, or to be told to children. The thirty-year-old mother and the sixteen-year-old daughter's boyfriend. The journey is paved with thorns and thistles of shame, gossip, and my father's silence. Perhaps his shame too; he's never said. How much does he know? My mother's promise to Eduardo was fulfilled—he arrived in Toronto within a year. My proxy marriage to him, at sixteen, only needed one signature. Simple. I stayed for over six years in a marriage so unwanted, I pretended I was single for a year

133

while dreaming of escape and love's ambrosia. I stayed until I walked out at twenty-two, never to return. Cupid offered me his golden cup in the rapturous gaze of Claudio's blue eyes.

But I say nothing of this to my cousins. I let them think I'm the hero, the winner, in this tawdry contest. I don't speak of freedom's price, the debt exacted by the cosmos. There's always a price, isn't there?

My father's visits and telephone calls ebbed to a stop through the years; I never again saw Manuelito. And when I least expect, just when laughter drowns out all other senses, the skinny girl with mollusks in her hair reemerges from the muddy depths of memory's river.

But tomorrow I'm flying back to Toronto; the Tejo left behind.

For now.

OIL PEOPLE

David Huebert

They are in the attic among the relics when Marc makes the offer. The birds gaze down in their dead-eyed hundreds; the cage of the hoop skirt ruffles on its stand. Jade always takes guests up here their first time—the attic teetering with Bankers Boxes, crates of journals, flaccid hardcovers, blasted drill bits, crude daguerreotypes. Out the window squats the red-brick museum building. Beyond it the ersatz fields, the jerker lines swaying, the engine churning in the pumphouse. If it were night they would see the glowing plants, thirty klicks away in Sarnia. If it were night they'd see flares.

I've done it five times, Marc says, squaring his shoulders. *Done it.* He wiggles. Marc is eleven, two full years older, but it is not his age that makes her wonder, nor the downy dark hair rashed around his lips. It's his sloe-eyed confidence, the tease of the storm in the window.

On the lawn below, new-hewn planks for the road, treated logs for the replica derricks. On the fringes of the property, the ceaseless rock of the jerker lines. She has seen the magazines in the soggy cardboard box on the low school roof. Trish boosted her up and together they clenched and stared at the raw clefts, spored pelvises.

Five times, he repeats.

What comes to mind is slugs, watching them shrivel and squirm in the lettuce patch as her father pours salt from the Windsor box.

In and out, he says. Simple.

Where?

He grins. Shows gums, membrane. The remnants of a lip tie. Right here, he says.

No. The bedroom.

Shh. He holds up a hand. Noise from the ladder. Feet on rungs.

Jackie's face appears, grinning in the hatch. She sets an elbow down, spins one of their mother's Marlboros. Marc stands panting, snub-nosed, open-mouthed. Jackie lights the Marlboro.

You shouldn't be smoking here.

Who's going to stop me? Pig Valves?

You shouldn't call him that.

Thanks. You two going to kiss or what?

Marc spins, ruffled. Thumps over to the ladder and stands there huffing. Jackie clears the ladder and Marc awkwards past her, pumps down the rungs.

Jackie glides up to the window, hitches her bra and exhales a soft luxury of smoke. Soon Marc appears among the lumber in his mud-stained Air Jordans, brochure crinkled in his hand. He lopes up the long drive, rat-tail bobbing past the geese and the dug well, through the jerker lines, beyond the museum. At last, he turns off toward Oil Heritage Way.

Wow, Jackie says, mock-shivering. Hot date.

At the Canadian Petroleum Legacy Museum, we use genuine nineteenth-century drilling technology to produce 20,000 barrels of crude annually. Using our "oil farming" technique, we drill day and night from 200 wells, all more than 100 years old. The Legacy Museum is a family business, run by the descendants of oil pioneer Clyde J. Armbruster, who drilled the first gusher in

Oil Springs and helped trigger the Lambton County oil rush of the 1860s. By the 1890s, Armbruster had become the most prolific oil producer in Canada. Come see the famous Canada Rig, watch the sway of our iconic jerker lines. Walk our fields to step into history and revisit this astonishing moment of global energy transition. Oil, illuminating the future!

Rain pelts the roof and a plastic bag zooms past the window. Something thumps in the fields. Jade tips and tilts, back and back, flirting with the edge. Chair, Phil says. Chair, her father says again. She comes down, confronts her dinner. Meat loaf with broccoli casserole.

The rain picks up to a gallop. Phil stands to get the buckets but her mother waves a hand. Don't worry, Laura says. They're already out. Even in the old wing? Laura smiles, shows the gap between her teeth. Jade chews meat loaf and tries not to think of beef, cows, grass, reactors. Her molars find a grain of gristle and she thinks of chicken livers in the grocery store, of the pig farm up the road. A story she heard once about dehorning, her uncle with bolt cutters in his hands, a dozen steer shooting blood from their heads.

Her parents talk guests, media, the bid. Her father gleams the words: "National Historic Site." Jackie serves herself salad and pushes it around her plate, brilliant with indifference. Her parents drone logistics and Jade's eyes land on the mantelpiece, Jackie's old prize bill. The purple ten, special issue from the Trudeau government, 1971. All the refineries gleaming, triumphal, wending train tracks, skyscrapers, the city on the hill.

Her father takes the Tabasco, showers his meat loaf. They sit listening to the wind croon, rain tock into buckets. Jackie pinkys ketchup, mentions the news, a story about radiation, the Chernobyl babies—her pet horror.

Stop, Laura says. She'll have nightmares again.

Jackie turns to Jade, hisses: Don't think you're safe.

Jade squirms. Safe from what?

Jackie turns hard on her little sister. Radiation, she says, doing ghoul-fingers. Chernobylings! You do know, Jackie says, coming closer. About the babies born with no ears. Kids with tiny useless arms. She mimes it, flailing chickenish.

Laura bristles, stands. Jackie rises, smiling, spins around. Clear your plate, missus. Jackie laughs, floats away, leaves Jade alone at the table, staring into the hot sauce, the Tabasco bottle, its glimmering fish-green necktie, the strange red glow of its core.

Jade knows that newborns have silver eyes, that babies cannot see colour. She's read about cesium-137, corium lava, bubbler pools. She knows about iodine fallout, xenon gas. She knows it is in the air, in the grass, in the cows, in the milk. On TV, she's seen the scorched building, the dipygus piglet, and the radiotropic fungi growing on the reactor walls. She knows about thyroid cancer, acute radiation syndrome. She knows about the doctors advising women to abort. And she knows how they claw at the gates of her dreams. Legions of babies. Babies with cloven hooves. Babies with fangs. Fingerless babies, babies with horns growing out of their eye sockets. Picket fences adorned with baby heads.

The storm takes out a few jerker line posts. Her father is up early to repair them. She watches from the window as he raises the mallet, thumbs his belt loops, worries his moustache, heads back to the shed. She thinks of his heart. She has a hard time picturing it, a pig's valve. Between thwacks, he looks up, sees her in the window of the old gothic home. She meets him in the kitchen, where he's boiling water for instant coffee.

Want a ride today?

Bus is fine. How bad is it?

Phil grins. Not the worst, he says, cupping her face in his thick hands. He kneels down beside her and cinches her onto a chair. Strokes her hair and puts an Eggo in the toaster. Pads the butter into the grids the way she likes. Then the syrup, how he always does it: a long-tailed serpent, a perfect S.

Sure, she says. A ride would be nice.

On her way across the schoolyard, she catches Marc's eye. He's standing on the hill where she lost a tooth last year, and when she passes he drops his gaze, comparing comics with Adam Saulnier. Maybe he's embarrassed. Maybe he's scared. Maybe he won't say anything.

At lunch she finds Trish. Dainty Trish with her rainbow scrunchies, perpetually rearranging her pencil case.

Only oil witches eat baloney, Adam Saulnier boors as he passes. You smell like burnt rubber.

Don't mind the spaz, Trish yells. Pig fucker!

The afternoon passes in Ancient Egypt, lessons on King Tut. On the bus home the kids ask if it was good for her. She glares at the chip bags in the ditches, bullet holes in the YIELD sign. How the world can pivot. How the muck can rise and thrash and seem to scream.

Was it good for you, Oil Witch?

The trees whiz by, the willows, the branches from the storm raked to the sides of the road. Bulrushes climb out of highway grit.

What're you talking about?

The blow job, Adam Saulnier says, jabbing a thumb at Marc. He mimes it, makes choking sounds. Jade curls into Trish, who glares back, mutters something about incest. I heard your sister plays the rusty trombone. I heard she's pregnant, got a change-ling. Adam whispers in Marc's ear, but Marc does not turn back. Sits pressed against the window, looking out. Jade stares into the back of Marc's rat-tailed head but he won't turn, won't meet her eyes.

Jade is watching a new show, *Teenage Mutant Teenage Ninja Turtles*. Her mother appears, hair freshly washed, curls drying.

She smells of coconut and nicotine. The turtles are breaking into the Technodrome, trying to return Master Splinter to his human form.

Laura sits down beside her girl, heaves her long-day sigh. She nods to the show. Aren't you a little old for this?

A pink brainy blob is lecturing Shredder. Jade considers explaining the backstory, her fascination, the story of a boy named Yoshi finding four baby turtles that had tumbled into a storm drain, then finding them crawling in a strange purple ooze that turned out to be a potent mutagen, mingling DNA with whatever creature it touched.

Instead, she shrugs. Are we poor people?

Her mother laughs. She does a little gesture around the land. We're not poor people. We're oil people.

In their house, this is a stock phrase. Yet she finds that she has never heard it in its realness, its music, its wonder. She thinks the phrase to herself, then speaks it wistful: Oil people.

Her mother smiles, flips her wet hair. That's right: it's in our blood.

Their parents go out and Jackie makes herself a drink, serves Jade a glass of orange juice and cackles as Jade rises, nauseous, and spits it in the sink, her mouth and throat a corrosion of vodka.

Jackie laughs, snorts. Sorry. It's too easy, you're too easy. Come back, she says. Jade approaches, sits gingerly on the far pole of the couch. Listen, she says, hitching her bra. You're growing up. It's not easy. It's mean. She shrugs, downs her screwdriver. Sometimes you get bitten. Sometimes you bite back.

The turtles are smashing droid heads together. In our blood, Jade thinks. She turns her pale arms over, examines the veins beneath her skin, that curious circuitry of blue.

Jade dreams the inside of a reactor. A wide-open hangar like a huge pool, knee-high water glowing computer blue. In the middle the great churning core. In the reactor there are needles, driving down, needles pumping through the floor, which, she sees now, is made of skin and flesh. An alarm starts to honk and blare and when she looks down she sees the skin floor opening, hinging open on a vague black underworld. She reaches down and dips her hands into the oil, drawing it up like black ink and when she looks at her hands again she finds them burnt, blackened. Her hands melted into lumps, smoking lumps, oozing together in the sticky black. Then the goo-hands grow little heads and start talking but she cannot hear because the alarm is blaring, raging, rising and she is clawing useless at the walls, trying to climb for the light but the sun turns bruise, darkens and shrivels until it's a pygmy prune, at its fringe a tiny necrotic tear.

Phil makes her Eggos, slides her orange juice. The butter melts in the grids, mixes with the syrup he's snaked on. Want a ride today? he asks, his mouth full of waffle. He has syrup in the corners of his pushbroom moustache. No thanks, she says, heading out through the dining room. Wait, he calls. Not hungry? She opens her backpack, slips the Tabasco in. No thanks, she says again, letting the mean into her voice. Her father appears holding the plate, the golden disks of the toaster waffles. I don't like those anymore.

Jade is drawing a lion—the hieroglyphic for L—when she sees him mince through the hall. She waits for him to pass, then excuses herself. Clipping her toenails on the desk, Mrs Arsenault nods her along. Jade drifts the hall, walking soft, careful not to squeak. Waiting outside the bathroom, she hears the shush of a urinal, the creak of a rusted faucet.

Whoa, Marc says. Is this about the bus? I didn't say anything.
She steps close.
Promise.
He's shuddering, the buffed hall gleaming black and maroon.
Do you still want to?

He swallows, hard. Here is the hinge. She's been relying on this moment. Here is his choice, the place where all rumours could swivel on him. Be brave, she thinks. Brave boy.

Yeah, he says.

She takes him by the hand, leads him down into the basement, slips with him into the janitor's closet. They stand among paint cans, filthy mop heads strung from rafter nails. Jade eyes the doorway, then nods down. Let's see it. He swallows hard. Slowly, he takes it out. Opens his palm and holds it as if counting change. Close your eyes, she says, and he does. The fluorescent lights click and hum. His eyeballs twitch under their lids.

She takes it in her hand and it shrinks, turtles. Quietly, she eases the bottle from her jacket pocket. No peeking, she says, and the corners of his mouth flicker. She peels back its little hat and starts to rub. It's a mutant, she realizes. Vein-clung, vermiculate. Its horrid vertical mouth opening as if to speak.

What is it?

You'll see, she says, rubbing quiet, calm. Rubbing gentle, soft, until he starts to squirm.

She walks home quick, trying to beat the bus. She cuts across the shoulder, into the ditch, over the soy field. She hustles down the hill through the snatch of woods, past the jerker lines and the curbed wells and into her room. Michael Jackson glares, reaches, his belt full of bondage loops. Katarina Witt gleams, sticking the double axel. Jade's fingers probe her forearm, set in. The phone is ringing, and then it is not. She hears her mother calling—Phil! Phil! Still in her room, Jade sees her mother in the kitchen, toeing the patch of burnt tile in the shape of a chicken. Her mother going stern, saying no, really, that couldn't be right. Her mother cupping the receiver, shouting for her father. Phil! Phil! Her mother will not say hot sauce or doctor or Marc Oliver. Jade's fingernails sink into pale forearm flesh, loose a few trembling beads. She touches the blood, gropes its gratitude of red. Closing her eyes, she sees a thousand babies, naked in glass hospital warming chambers, their eyes fused shut. Twitching, spasming, crying. She hears footsteps, her mother. In perfect unison, the babies' eyelids snap open. All the same—their eyes wretched, red. All looking at her, watching her, seeing her. All their lily mouths blooming open at once to tell her it's in our blood, in our blood, our blood.

TIDES

Sara Freeman

On the long bus journey out, she doesn't cry or even have a single thought that she can name. She watches the dark impossibility of the road instead, the mostly empty seats ahead of her, the head of a woman a few rows up, listing forward and then jolting back. She does not sleep. She wants to be awake to make her declaration at the border. She will show her passport and when they ask, Where to? she will say without hesitation, The sea.

She does not have to leave. No one says: *You must go.* No clothes thrown out the window, no eviction notice. Her husband is already gone by then; she was the one to tell him that he had to go. She could say it was the baby—her brother's and his wife's. His sweet squawking through the open window in the apartment beneath hers. She could no longer live in this fixed way: their joy so firmly lodged beneath her grief. She could say that.

The motel advertises an ocean breeze but is nowhere near the beach. She waits in the small room, for something, for someone. She has turned her phone off, but she still feels it in her palm, waiting to bleat back to life. To deliver what message? *I love you. I miss you. Come back.* She left a note for her brother and his wife. No explanation or apology. *I'll be fine!* That's what she wrote. She asks at the reception desk about another motel, nearer the water this time. The woman behind the counter has eyebrows like tadpoles swimming lazily across her forehead. She says there is a town she might like, remote, for rich folks mostly, about thirty miles up the coast. There is a hostel there too. She puts her index finger on a map, her nail filed down to a tidy point. This one is canary yellow, the surrounding ones sky blue.

She gets a ride from a man who is delivering ice across the state. His eyes are blue and inflamed, his hands raw and meaty. The town sign reads: THIS ROAD LEADS TO ROME, with an ugly drawing of the Colosseum, followed by the population, 2,353. When she gets out in the town's central square, she touches the hard shell of the truck with gratitude and it is so cold, the hairs on her arm stand up.

There is no colosseum in this Rome. Instead, a supermarket, a Greek restaurant, an Italian restaurant, a seafood spot, an ice cream shop, a wine store, a laundromat, a pub, an inn, a garden centre, a health centre, a hardware store, a library, a clothing store, a pharmacy, a marina, and a dump.

The sea, in this new town, is surprisingly hard to get to. It is somehow everywhere and nowhere. She needs an invitation, a private viewing: through the stately homes, and onto the other side, where everything is vast and pristine. The other her, the one she left behind, would have easily slid between the giant piles, past the outdoor furniture, past the slim lounging bodies and their purebred dogs. Everything belonged to her then; that was back when she believed that nothing that could so easily be had wasn't somehow already hers.

From her bedroom window in the hostel, she can see it best: the sea and its expanse, edging in and then pulling back. She doesn't want to be in it yet. It is warm out, but she still feels frozen, blood-let, fleshless. She is content, for now, to watch the comings and goings from afar.

In the evenings, she walks along the town's main drag. It is shaped like a horseshoe. She often sees the same faces twice, on the way to the ice cream shop, and then on their way back. There are often tears on the return journey, mostly children's, but on one occasion a grown woman's and her wife's. Once desire is met, she thinks, there is only turning back from it. There is not much to do or see in the town at night: just tourists dining al fresco, prodding swordfish slabs and slurping oysters. A busker nearby crooning, *Oh, oh, Mexico*, as if he might be in this town in error. The first nights, she stops and finds a place among the small crowd gathered before him. But one evening, mid-song, he looks up and greets her with a complicit nod. Now, when she hears the busker's familiar sound, she passes by without so much as looking up.

She asks around at the hostel, and they tell her she is right: the prettiest beaches are cut off by the houses. It wasn't always like this, they say, the coastline so private and all. Some of the richest families used to turn a blind eye, but not anymore. In a few weeks, once the season is over, then that's a whole different story. For now there's the public beach, of course, but that's nothing to write home about. That's good, because she's not planning to write home about anything. They laugh, hearing her say this, and she thinks for a moment that nothing much has changed: she can say a few words in the right order and get people to love her for a moment.

She finds it, flanked by the supermarket and the garden center: a slip of public sand. There is an orange tent set up at the far end of the beach and two pairs of swollen, mangled feet sticking out. When she walks by, the screen is zipped halfway down, so that she can't see any faces, she can only hear the syncopated sound of their snoring.

She wonders what she will do when the money runs out. The thought is sticky, the first one like this, insisting on its own importance. It seems absurd somehow, that she must think of it, make something of this thought. The beach ends and there is a large expanse of dark, jagged rocks. She walks across the fraught ground, canvas shoes sliding dangerously beneath her. She slips and catches herself then slips again and falls hard on the rock. Not pain, just the feeling of everything coming up from within. She sits there, looking around, for someone, a witness to her fall, a hand to grip as she steadies herself back up. But there is no one, just the dome of orange light tented in the distance.

She buys a large lemonade filled with crushed ice and drinks it until her teeth and brain are numb. She shuts her eyes hard and when she opens them again, she is surprised to find that everything is still there: the lemonade truck, a few waves quietly churning in the distance, the sand, dank and gray, waiting to be touched.

She wakes one morning, clutching her stomach. No time has passed; her husband is by her side. He touches her rounded stomach with his palm. *Nearly there*, he says, speaking into her belly button. She is awake now, her palm on her own skin, the fingers cold and thin. Her belly is nearly concave, more than empty. She has been gone for three days, maybe four, or maybe it is six, and since then she has eaten a sleeve of saltines, some peanut butter from a spoon, a few beers, a lemonade, some fries and some licorice. She is saving money; she doesn't have much left. One thousand seven hundred and thirty-three. If she needs more, she'll turn the phone on, write her brother a message. He has never said no to her before. His only sister. She'll write to him and say something like this: *I am changing.* Or better yet: *I have changed.*

She sees children everywhere, in the flesh, but also in what they leave behind: striped swimsuits hanging over banisters and beach chairs, colourful pails discarded on the beach. When she sees them, children and their traces, she turns her head away. It is her head that does the turning. She speaks, as though defending herself before a jury: *This* is not about *that.*

At the town's small marina, day trippers clump around the seafood spot, composing their seaside shots: plush pink lobster rolls, heaped French fries snapped from above. In the background, a row of handsome wooden yachts, sterns wagging; a fisherman, sun-creased and smoking, unloading his mid-August catch. She doesn't stay long; the smell here makes her queasy. Fish entrails and sunscreen, cooking oil reused one time too many.

In a shop window along the main drag, she spots a letterpress sign: KEEP ROME OFF THE MAP. In this town, the patrician crowd don their modesty like a crown: beat-up station wagons, worn-in khakis, styles from thirty years past.

The diner here is famous for its 1950s memorabilia. She sits at the counter and orders the lumberjack special. She pictures a lumberjack laying her across his lap, breaking her, like a twig, in half. She eats a sausage link and one of three sunny-side-up eggs, a bit of the pancake just for the mouthful of syrup. This diner, with its defunct Coke machines and jukeboxes and old graphic lunch boxes, reminds her of her mother's house, crammed with dangerous nostalgia. A woman and her toddler sit nearby. She spoons cereal into his wet little mouth. He dribbles and she wipes. He dribbles and she wipes. Easy as that. The woman is wearing all linen and a large-brimmed hat; she looks old to be a mother. But who is she to say who is old and who is not? She was thirty-five when she got pregnant, thirty-six when she lost her child. And now she feels one hundred, or maybe only seven years old. She looks a moment too long. Something passes between them, the mother and her, a warm current of it: pity, or maybe its cousin, contempt. When she asks for the bill the man at the counter, pointing to the table where the mother and son were sitting, says, *They said to say good luck.*

In the bathroom mirror, she lets herself look up. She sees what the woman must have seen: the gaunt face, the hair matted to one side, the lips chapped, the nails bitten to the quick. She splashes cold water on her face and pulls her hair back. She looks nearly dead. *This* is not *that.* She looks down at her clothes; they are dirty but intact.

It is hot. The hottest day yet. August, slinking into September. Still hot by the evening, when the sun is a red face dipping its chin into the water. The public beach is empty. Everyone is on their patios sipping Campari and eating pistachios, saying their farewells. She removes her canvas shoes, her jeans and shirt, and moves into the water—sharp and cold as a knife's edge. She swims out until, when she turns her head, she can no longer make out her clothes bundled up on the sand, just a single line of darkness in the background. The water is bitter now, the moon just a sliver in the night, barely any comfort at all. She is that sliver, she thinks, drowning in the dark. She could die here, so slight and sinking. Nothing but her body to buoy her up. Whatever reserves she had, she has lost them now. She feels a rush of heat around her, her own urine, terror at her own thoughts. She thrashes around, trying to turn back, but even this turning, this changing course, seems impossible: the body has forgotten how to lead. It takes an eternity to move against the current, the arms and legs dumb with disuse and then too much exertion. She kicks hard, and then softer, it is easier this way, without trying at all; she is moving forward and back, lulled by the waves. She is like this forever, until she hits something, a rock, and then her knees hit it too, and she finds that she can crawl. Beneath her, the hard, wet certainty of the ground. She manages to get to her feet, finds her clothes in their pile, falls asleep in a damp heap.

She wakes before the sun and sits up, stiff and cold. She has always wanted this: To slip beneath the surface, to dispossess herself. Now that she has done it, it is hard to remember how her self could have become such a bottomless pit: feed me, fuck me, fill me, love me.

This is what it feels like to slip, she remembers telling her husband, when she was teaching him to ice skate on the Ottawa canal. *You can't teach someone how to slip.* He was right: you slip and then you've slipped and so you know.

Sometimes, she pictures them: her brother and his wife, discussing her now that she is gone. *Impossible*, that's what they would say. Or maybe, instead, *Beyond repair*.

The management has moved her things. *You were gone for two nights*, they tell her. She can only remember one, but she doesn't want to fight. Her things include: a toothbrush, a sweater, two T-shirts, one pair of jeans, the biography of a famous chef, all stuffed inside an old backpack with her brother's initials embroidered on it: *P.S.T.* They have placed her in the large dormitory. She can tell from the work boots neatly lining the beds that the place is full of men. She buys a six-pack of beer and some cigarettes and brings them with her to the beach. She will wait until the men are sleeping before climbing back into her cot. She lies down. The beer and cigarettes are effective; she feels herself drifting pleasantly into the night. Today she has only eaten half a packet of tea cookies and a banana. The waves are loud, brimming over, coursing to their violent metre. Before she falls asleep, she thinks: This is what babies must hear when they are held inside the womb.

She wakes to a hand on her shoulder, a gruff one, a man's hand, shaking her awake. A light so bright she can't make a thing out, only voices, two of them, ordering her to stand up. She is on the beach, her hand clutching at wet sand. Her eyes adjust and she sees them: two men in uniform. Father figures, she thinks. She smiles up at them. They don't smile back. Bad daddies. She says something out loud, but it sounds more garbled than what she had in her head. They grab her, one arm and then the other, not at the armpit, but by the wrists, as though she were just a kid. Swing me around and around and around and around. But it hurts, the joints are no longer loose; they are fixed in place. *You're hurting me*, she says, this time clearly. *I'm not doing anything wrong.* They point to the empty beer cans, more of them than she can remember drinking. She tries to explain: there were men in the hostel, she was just waiting for them to fall asleep. She is sitting in the back seat of their car now, hands cuffed. They have forgotten to put her seat belt on. The metal beneath the seat hits her tailbone, a familiar, pummelling beat. She has never been this cold, this brittle, her entire body caught up in a single spasm. *I'm still scared*, she says, at the door of the hostel: a giant mouth, gaping open. She begs the fat officer to take her inside, sit with her until she falls asleep, but he tells her, *Grow up, lady*, and takes his leave. Inside, all the men are sleeping, quiet as babies. She falls asleep quickly. When she wakes, she looks around and all the men are already gone.

The men are here for the season: blueberries, raspberries, blackberries. Three of them are working on a house. *The house is so big*, she hears one of them say in Spanish, *you could fit my whole village inside of it.*

They are kind, concerned for her. They say, *Güera, qué pasó?* pointing to her clothes, her shoes. She tells them, *Nada*, nothing has happened. They let her in on their talk. She likes being near them; she understands one in five words, this is enough.

She is like a ball being passed from one set of hands to another, none of them holding on for too long. In the communal kitchen, one offers her tortillas with beans, the other spaghetti from a can; another gives her cookies mortared with jam and vanilla cream. In the mornings, she wakes with them before dawn. They eat white bread slick with margarine, and make her Nescafé their special way: they heat the milk and let the granules dissolve, then add two heaping spoonfuls of sugar. The older one says: *Mija, tienes que comer*, and makes her eat a second piece of Wonder Bread sloppy with supermarket jelly.

One evening, she sees a few of the men huddled around the kitchen table, hunched over the cracked screen of a phone. In miniature, she makes out a penis sliding between two breasts as taut and playful as helium balloons. They turn the screen off as soon as they see her. They disperse, scatter back into the dormitory.

The young one asks her: *Cómo te llamas?* She tells him without much thought: *Nada*. She likes it as a name, *Nada*. The girls who work at the reception desk think it's strange: how much time she spends with the men, sitting and biting her nails, not talking at all. One morning, she finds her few clothes at the foot of her bed, folded and washed.

Sometimes, in the evenings, they watch a movie on the small television hanging from the ceiling. They all have to crane their necks to see the tiny men on the screen dangling from helicopters and saving women from burning buildings. Sometimes when she gets bored by the action, she walks around and picks up their empty beer cans, rinses them, arranges them neatly by the bin.

For the first time in her life, she does not dream.

In the middle of the night, she hears the young one in his bed. His moans are so low and muffled, she feels as though they are coming from her, a rush of blood in her own veins, a throbbing at her own throat. Not so long ago, she might have slipped out of bed, slid her hand between his legs and told him: *Let's try this instead.* The sound makes way for another, not sex but slow, withheld sobs, those of a much littler boy. Her body is stiff with remorse. She has no rounded edges anymore, no warmth to proffer him.

In the morning, she finds it hard to look at him. She pours him his cereal instead, his milk, dunks a spoon in it. *Aquí tienes.* He boasts about a girlfriend, a toddler back home. Two years, six months, three weeks, and a day: This is how long it's been since he's seen them last. He is thick and strong and still growing, his front teeth too big for his mouth. She wants to touch the down on the upper lip and say, *There, there.*

She counts backward, tries to do her own dismal math. August, July, June, May, April, March. Five months since she saw her own child, eyes stuck shut, limp as an unclenched fist.

James Taylor is gone, but Joan Baez is there to replace him. She sings a song called *Colorado*, in which the only lyric is *Colorado*, repeated over and then over again. When she thinks the song is over, Joan begins again: *Colorado ... Colorado*. In Canada, where she is from, no one ever sings songs about Alberta.

The season is nearly done. She lets the fact of it wash over her. The city folks have gone home, the hostel will close. She hears it but the words are water and she a gripless surface, a flat expanse. The day arrives and the men are all packed up. *I miss you*, she tells them in Spanish. She doesn't know the future tense for *miss*. There is a van here to pick them up. She stands outside, nose running, waving, a single arm wrapped around her for warmth, a mother sending her boys off on the school bus.

The girls at the reception desk tell her she's got one day to clear out. They feel sorry for her, but they are only teenagers. *Senior year*, they say to her like a question and an answer all rolled into one. She tries to turn her phone back on, but the screen stays dark, every crevice filled with sand.

They tell her that if she helps them clean the place, she can stay three more nights. She vacuums and mops the floors, cleans the toilets and the scum between the tiles. She covers the furniture with tarps. She cleans the kitchen, consolidates all the half-eaten boxes of spaghetti into a single Ziploc bag. In the lost and found, she finds three dresses and two sarongs, a hot plate and a nightlight, an elegant fountain pen with the two parts of the nib violently split apart. The three of them collect 168 dollars' worth of coins, under the beds, inside the couches, in the laundry room under the machines. The girls whisper to one another and sheepishly offer her twenty dollars in dimes. She finds a lighter with a woman's silhouette on it. When it is upright, the woman wears a pretty pink dress. When she flips it upside down, the woman bares her ample breasts, a tassel, mid-twirl, on each nipple. During their lunch break, she sits in the sun and flips the lighter up and then down, up and then down again. The girls place a paper plate at her feet, a hot dog adorned with two perfect stripes: one red, one gold.

Three hundred and twenty-three dollars. This is counting the twenty dollars in dimes.

The three days are up. *Just one more night*, she begs. The girls hesitate, convene privately. *Fine*, they say, *but tomorrow morning you're gone, or else we're going to have to call the boss.* The next afternoon, they find her, still asleep in the cavernous room. *He's coming now*, they warn her. *He knows about you and he is displeased.* They use this word, *displeased*, as though it is a word she might not have heard before. They lay it on thick. They took a chance on her and now she's going to have to pay. She was their age once, sharpening herself against her own blunt force. And so she tells them she's very sorry, gives them fifty dollars, and buys them a six-pack each before taking her leave.

There are just hours left before sundown. Her backpack is heavy with hostel gleanings; the weight bears down on her shoulders, right down into her heels. Maybe she'll sleep on the public beach; she thinks of the tent, the mangled feet. She buys an ice cream cone, soft vanilla sprinkled with a messy hand. She walks along the main street, not thinking, every mouthful too sweet. She takes inventory of her skills. The list is short and so, easy to remember.

That evening in the pharmacy, she buys soap, razors, shampoo, and a cheap bottle of perfume. Mascara in a bright pink tube, a plum-red lipstick, foundation one grade of beige too dark—every item the cheapest she can find. She pays twenty dollars for a day pass at the health club. She asks how much for just a shower. *There's no price for that, miss.* She washes her hair, once, twice, three times, each strand stiffened with salt

and grease. She looks down from time to time. She doesn't recognize the body beneath: feral, bleak. She shaves everything
off. She forgot to ask for a towel so she walks around naked,
drying herself off. She clips her nails and plucks her eyebrows,
brushes her teeth. Two women in their sixties walk past her,
catch a glimpse; she is denuded, goosebumped, a chicken with
her feathers just off. They stare down sheepishly at her feet.
She slips on one of the dresses from the hostel's lost and found.
Floral, cheap. She is tall, and this spaghetti-strapped shift for
someone shorter; it sits too high on her thighs. In the mirror,
she sees what she will look like to others: she is not displeased.
Only she knows what is amiss, like a loose tooth at the back
of her mouth holding on by just a few threads. From time to
time, she touches the fact of it with her tongue.

He is easy enough to spot. He orders a beer before the last one
is halfway done. Rich boy, she thinks, hair smoothed back,
gold pinky ring nestled in flesh. Prep school, financier, end-of-
season loaf. She sits next to him. His teeth are small, his gums
inflamed. He is already gone, left the building. She doesn't want
money, she tells him, just a house to hole up in, a bed for the
night. She takes his hand; she feels the fat pooling at the knuckles. She wonders if he ever takes the ring off, if he can. No, she
doesn't do drugs, not that kind. *It's a real problem around here*,
he says, in his newscaster's drone.

He is not a bad guy, she thinks, just a dummy, a clown. The ice
clanks against his teeth, the cold sinks through her. She asks
him to take his blazer off, to let her wear it. She is chilled to the
bone, she tells him, dying of cold. He takes his wallet out of the
inside pocket, flips it open. Now, he'll show her his sweetheart,
she thinks. But he takes out his own college ID and points to
the picture: *I want you to see what I looked like when I was
sober*. In the photograph, he is good-looking, slim-faced,
jaw pressed proudly out. Now there is one large fold of fat in

which his face is propped up. She takes his hand and places it on her lap. She doesn't mind. This is the easy stuff.

She was the one who taught herself to read. *B* and *A* makes *BA*. Everyone asked her, incredulous, *How did you do that?*

He lists back and falls off his stool, takes her with him. She is lying above him: flotation device, emergency raft. It takes a long time for the patrons to turn their heads, to witness the wreckage. She gets off him and pulls at his hand, but he is heavy, dead weight at the bottom of a slippery rope. *He's bleeding*, she says, and three big men come to hoist him up.

Such a pretty house, she says, despite herself. It's his parents' house. Large enough so he can lumber up the back stairs without waking them up, a house designed around its blind spots. She remembers a talk she attended when she was in her early twenties. *The Architecture of Estrangement*. She had liked the title, but the talk itself had been garbled, a series of simple words at the mercy of impossible sentences.

She doesn't know what she has in mind. One night, negotiated into two. She'll lie down, open up, the nib of a fountain pen split neatly apart. He has regained some strength. He looks over at her on the landing, has forgotten how he got here, who she is. He tells her she ought to go. But then he lays his hand on her breast and says: *Fuck ... well, fuck.*

In the room, there are two twin beds, which he insists on pushing together. *I'm a gentleman*, he informs her. *You had me fooled*, she says. She lies down, closes her eyes, falls into shallow sleep: She is in a wading pool, filling a red plastic cup with water and pouring it back out. Happy as a clam. She likes to watch the water moving with her, draining out over the lip of the plastic tub. *You taste so good*, he tells her, his mouth wet, a dog lapping water up from its bowl. Salt and sand and sea urchins, she thinks, and the vanilla crap she spritzed at the waistband of her undies. How did she know to do that? *B* and *A* is *BA*. Just like that. He crouches over her; she opens her mouth just wide enough to let him in. This is what he tastes like: dirty dog, pickled organs, ashtray, grout.

She wakes up, throat dry, head in her mouth. The two beds have slid slowly apart, the man crucified on one, she clammed inward on the other. The last thing she remembers is his slim dick prying open her mouth. She rolls onto her side: one leg down and then another. She is jelly, the room a spinning top. She finds her backpack, rummages through it, puts on her pants, a shirt that is clean enough. His wallet is on the ground; a ten and three ones. She leaves the ten and takes the ones, then takes the ten and leaves the ones. She could wait for him to wake up, big boy in his tiny bed. She could stroke his head, beg him for a few more nights. But *this* cannot be *that*, she thinks. She returns to the wallet, takes the university ID and slides it into her pocket. He should know better: there is no way back to the past.

It is early in the town. Earlier than she thought. The stores are shut, the air still cool from the night. The gulls sway and swerve. They land on the lips of garbage cans, tipping beaks into wide-open mouths. She would not say: *I am hungry.* She might say: *I feel like a trash can emptied out.*

She used to say to her husband, if she can still call him that: *Not feeling is a feeling too.*

DOI MOI BEANS

Philip Huynh

In many ways my parents never left each other, although here we were in Vancouver while my mother was buried back in Vietnam. My father kept a black-and-white picture of her on top of our television set. Every evening he saved a portion of his dinner and made an offering to her. Occasionally he spoke to her in the dark when he was alone. From my bedroom in our little apartment, on the edge of sleep, I could hear the rhythm of my father's voice through the walls, although I could never make out the words.

My father remained a committed bachelor, though he met women every day at the diner that he worked at on Southeast Marine Drive. Such as the old ladies that came in every morning, long retired but still wearing their blue, red, or violet work suits with shoulder pads, now a size too large because of their dwindling frames. Or the young mothers who came in with their unwieldy strollers which my father never failed to trip over. Or the teens who came after school and ordered their milkshakes without whipped cream, atonally tapping their heels against the metal bar stool while waiting for boyfriends at hockey practice.

All the women he knew were regulars, but at what point they first entered my father's life, and at what point they decided to stay, he could never tell. Except for one. One night at closing a woman walked into the diner, out of the rain, alone. She wore a white blouse, white pants, and a thin necklace that brought out the silver in her eyes. A cobalt-blue belt. Her name was Auburn, which was the colour of her hair.

"Are you open?" she asked. There were no other customers. My father was wiping down the counters and had already cleaned out the grill. He was tired and would have pointed late customers out the door, usually raucous kids on a pit stop after the clubs. But by the bags under her eyes, she seemed interested in nothing but a bite to eat.

He waved her in.

"Are you sure?" she said. "You look closed."

"Not a problem," said my father. He gave her the menu, a sheet of cardboard folded down the middle and coated in plastic, announcing typical diner fare.

"Your first time here?"

"I drive by all the time," she said. "But I've never stopped in before."

"I would have known if you had," said my father, in his nonchalantly earnest manner that made the woman think nothing of the comment. "I never forget a face."

"Nor do I," said Auburn. She put down the menu. "You know, I think I'll just have a coffee, if that's still possible."

"Of course," said my father. In fact, the coffee tanks were already emptied and the filters cleaned of grounds. If he made another batch it would be enough for twenty customers. My father went to his locker where he kept a small coffee maker for his personal use. He pulled out a small bag of beans which he had ground himself—his own personal bag that he bought from an Italian grocer on Fraser Street. A good cup of coffee and a cigarette were his luxuries. He couldn't bear to drink the mud water that his diner served.

Auburn asked for the coffee black. "Working late?" asked my father.

"I'm afraid so," she said. She had brought a slim leather briefcase with her, but before she opened it she took a sip of the coffee. Her eyes widened as if she had just inhaled smelling salts. She focused on the white china cup in front of her, as if to brace herself from vertigo.

"Where did you get this?" she asked.

"Is there something wrong with it?"

She laughed. "No, there's nothing wrong with it. It's not what I expected to find here."

My father bristled at this truth. "We serve only the finest," he said.

"You must. I know the farmer who cultivated these beans."

"You are in the coffee business?" said my father.

"I am."

"You don't look like a farmer."

"I'm a broker, actually."

"A coffee broker," said my father. "You must sell only the best."

"I don't want to brag."

He put on his best smile, and put his finger on the menu. "Order something," he said. "You look starved."

Auburn smiled politely. "I guess I should." She ordered a grilled cheese sandwich and a garden salad. "It's the buying season. I haven't had a wink of sleep in two nights."

"Is that right?"

She lifted her cup. "You do have good taste. Are you a buyer as well?"

"I had my own plantation," he said. "In Vietnam."

Auburn arched her eyebrows. She had a clear cartography of the world of coffee, and they included such places as Brazil and Chile, Yemen and Sumatra. Vietnam was terra incognito for her.

My father smiled. "Vietnam is a hidden paradise for coffee," he said. "And now that America has lifted the embargo, the world will discover it again."

"Like an Atlantis," said Auburn. "Waiting to emerge from its depths." She licked the oil of the cheese from her fingers.

"There's money to be made," he said. "That's all there is to it."

When she was done my father refused her the bill. "Come back," he said. "You won't be disappointed."

My father came home that night and didn't sleep. Instead he made himself a cup of coffee from a stash of beans that he kept in the highest kitchen cupboard, where he hid his most valuable possessions from me since I was small, even though I was now taller than him by a head.

The smell of the coffee quickly filled our small apartment, pungent and spicy, a smell of the rainforest and red peppers. My father asked me if I wanted a cup.

"No thanks," I said. But it was too late to say no. The coffee was already brewing. "Don't let this go to waste," he said. "It's your heritage."

The taste of the coffee jolted me awake. "You're kidding," I said.

My father nodded. They were the beans from my father's old plantation. Among all the crampness in our apartment, in the jungle of toiletries and clothes and junk, in the corners of drawers and shelves, sometimes lay something worth keeping.

"How did you get this?" I asked.

My father smiled. "I have connections everywhere, even to the past."

We sat down in the living room. We never drank coffee together. I had the television on, but turned it to Mute. My father told me about his encounter with Auburn.

"So you met another businessperson," I said.

"Yes. A coffee broker," said my father. "She buys from all over the world, but she doesn't know Vietnam." He was in his own sweet thoughts, sipping coffee, wondering aloud about who this woman knew. "Maybe Murchie's, maybe Blenz," he said, referring to the local coffee chains that served a decent cup.

The plantation was in the mountains north of Saigon. It was founded by the Jesuits, owned by my father's father, then passed down to my father, who left it briefly with my mother for "safekeeping" when my father and I left Vietnam just before the Communists came. My mother was supposed to join us when my father and I properly established ourselves in Canada. But long before he made enough money, the Communists took over South Vietnam and my mother passed away. My father thought that the plantation had been converted into a commune and that it would be the last he would hear of it, until he started receiving letters from Mr Pham, one of my mother's uncles. Mr Pham had taken over the plantation with the Communists' blessing. My father was relieved that the estate remained in the family and was still operating, as tenuous as his tie to Mr Pham was. Most of the coffee was being shipped to the Soviet Union.

Every year my father would receive in the mail a small package containing a sample of the year's harvest. In return my father would send to Mr Pham a postcard—of Vancouver's downtown haloed by mountains, or of Gassy Jack's clock in Gastown, or the gardens at Queen Elizabeth Park. For Mr Pham, these postcards were his only missives from the Western world, and were as good as one of the Statue of Liberty to inflame his fantasies of capitalism. My father always wrote of his personal progress in "the food industry" in these postcards, although what he meant by the "food industry" and "progress" was always left to interpretation. My father always signed off with a vague but tantalizing promise that someday the two men would do business together.

Meanwhile, Auburn failed to reappear. For the next two weeks my father kept the lights on after closing time, leaving one burner ready in case Auburn showed up late. He became more convinced that she was just an illusion in his head. He could only remember her as a constellation of twinkling details, an ivory barrette holding her hair, a gently upturned nose when she tasted the cup of coffee, the perfect symmetry of the V formed by her elbows as she held the cup to warm her hands, which made an hourglass with the reflected V of her crossed legs.

But after a fortnight she arrived, once again, in the rain. She was dressed as exquisitely as before, although small bags had formed under her eyes like the day's silt. The rain had loosened a few strands of her hair from a braid.

"Are you open?" she asked.

My father smiled. "For you, yes. Coffee?"

She sat down on a stool, slightly slumped. "Yes, I'm afraid I will need one."

My father had brought along Mr Pham's beans. Once he got his personal coffee maker to start percolating, he came out to the counter to watch her. She had a document neatly set out on the counter, next to a small calculator.

"You are like that famous song," said my father.

He had seemed to break Auburn out of deep thought, and she looked up at him puzzled.

"It's been a hard day's night," he said.

He was able to tease out a slight smile from her. "One that won't end," she said. "It's been a rough season."

My father was familiar with those. Seasons when there was too much rain, seasons when there was not enough.

"A finicky harvest?" he asked.

"Not as finicky as the customers," said Auburn. "It's been chaos with all the Starbucks opening up here. They are even penetrating Commercial Drive. It's made everyone rather desperate."

"Fair trade labelling seems to be a possibility," she went on, almost to herself. "Although it hasn't really made it up here yet. Like everything, it's about being ahead of the curve. Being a broker used to be a simple thing. I used to just buy and sell coffee. Now I'm part marketing strategist and part shrink." Starbucks had changed Auburn's vocabulary. Conversations with her clients about gardens and even literature were being replaced by marketing talk. My father listened intently. He pictured a world of oak drawing rooms in the British Properties, of cedar patios with views of the Pacific Ocean, where Auburn would sip coffee and advise an old doyenne about the changing world below, listening to the doyenne's end-of-empire anxieties, like watching ivy grow on a manor in benign disrepair.

Listening to Auburn, my father had forgotten the percolating coffee until he could smell it. He brought her a cup, black. All he could do was to hold the china saucer with both hands to prevent it from shaking.

He pretended to clean out the stove while Auburn took her first sip. Her face, which had had an expression of dreaminess lined with weary, was suddenly wiped clear of expression. She took another sip. Then another. Her jaw hardened and she pulled away from the cup.

"Where did you get this coffee?" she asked.

"You don't like it?" asked my father.

"I've never tasted it before," she said.

"I've tasted everything."

It was his turn to draw Auburn into his world, of a plantation at the base of the evergreen mountains, of a French Vietnam before the war. That this coffee had not been shared more widely was deep down on a long list of casualties of the war, but it was a casualty nonetheless.

Auburn took one last sip of the coffee. "I can't have any more of it," she said. "Not tonight." Auburn asked my father just to give her the regular dregs, along with a grilled cheese sandwich.

My father drank the rest of the coffee alone at his locker after she left. He knew he would see her again. The Clinton administration had recently lifted America's trade embargo against Vietnam. This was a rare moment in the annals of business, when pent-up demand was matched by pent-up supply.

Auburn now dropped in regularly and would ask for the "Vietnamese blend," as she called it. My father would tell her that he would have to check to see if there was any left, knowing full well that the stash had remained untouched since the last time she had come. She told my father that it would be a sin not to share this coffee more widely.

No terms were decided between him and Auburn, and yet my father felt that he needed to act quickly, as if to stay ahead of the global political winds. He bought a phone card.

Mr Pham was already selling beans to Russia, to Italy, and recently to France. It was just a matter of time before he would break into the North American market. How much did my father want?

"I'm not the buyer," said my father. "I'm a broker."

"So you know some big fish, heh?"

"I know some big fish," said my father.

"Good," said Mr Pham. "Lead me to them."

Auburn would come just after my father turned over the hanging OPEN sign in the front door. She came tired, preoccupied, and my father could tell that she wasn't tasting her food when she chewed it. But she'd come—even when my father was out of his Vietnamese blend. She drank and ate whatever my father put in front of her. My father gave her salads and plates served on whole wheat bread. He tried to wean her off the fried stuff.

And then sometimes she came in fresh and bright-eyed, as if she had wakened from a nap. On those evenings she had on makeup as if she had put it on just for him.

My father spoke of me and of my mother. Auburn told my father that she was a widow as well, but with no children. She seemed to take an interest in me, or at least the idea of me—the fact that I had aspirations in both acting and in business.

"What an interesting convolution your son is," she said.

"It must be difficult, to not have any children to remember your husband by," said my father.

I would often be asleep when my father came home. Nights when I couldn't sleep we would watch TV together with the volume turned off. He talked about Auburn purely as a business opportunity, but nights when she didn't show up to the diner he would come home and sulk, with so much nothing to say.

One night, between sips of coffee, she asked, "Would you like to come to dinner?" My father asked her to repeat the question.

"We should discuss business," she said. "You've been feeding me all this time, I should at least return the favour. Bring your son."

They arranged to meet on Friday. Auburn left my father a business card with her address. She worked out of the home. Later that night he put the card on my knee while I was watching TV. He told me I would be putting a suit on. We were going to a business dinner. This was Wednesday night. Over the next two days he didn't say much to me. He sent his best suit to the cleaners even though it had been in its garment bag for years. He spent a lot of time talking on the phone with Mr Pham, going through a bunch of phone cards. I picked up the used cards in the random spaces where my father left them in the apartment—on the kitchen table, on the couch, on the floor. I threw them away.

My father came home early from work on Friday to change. We were both spiffed up in suits with our hair slicked back. We even took a cab. My father didn't want to take our Corolla. My father showed the business card to the cab driver, as if Auburn's address could not be communicated in any other way than in gold print.

The apartment building was a nondescript concrete high-rise, typical 1970s Vancouver. Nothing looked remarkable about the shiny parkade lobby, or the rickety elevator to the fourteenth floor, or the silver doorbell on the white door.

Auburn opened the door, smiled, and let us in. She offered me her hand, palm down, and I shook it, not sure if that was the right thing to do. She winked at me and led us in. Her apartment occupied a vast floor space, maybe the entire floor. The living room windows had an unobstructed view of the North Shore mountains and the inlet below. This was Vancouver as it really was, but as I had never seen it. My father was quiet. He acted as if he and Auburn were strangers, and stared at the floor or over her shoulder instead of eye to eye. He didn't trust her when she told him it was okay to keep his shoes on. He took his shoes off and made me take mine off as well.

Auburn, in a slinky black dress with her hair done up in a braid, was of a piece with her surroundings. At the time, the only way I could describe the apartment was that it belonged to someone who had money. Now, I can say that it wasn't your typical wealthy Vancouver apartment. For one thing, she had furniture that was older than the city itself. She gave us a tour of the living room, of the Victorian armchairs that she had bought at auction, of the Steinway piano in the corner that had been shipped in from New York. Her walls were covered with master paintings—Van Gogh's *Sunflowers*, Monet's *Water Lilies*, Caravaggio, Vermeer. They were perfect reproductions that she got from Europe, down to the brushstrokes and even the frames.

My father, for his part, sat stiffly on the couch. He declined every drink she offered—Riesling, beer, Scotch, tea—until she raised water like a white flag. I was happy to take her up on her offer of Scotch. I had never tasted it before.

"I have a Brora, aged thirty years. Best of the Highlands."

"You shouldn't," said my father. "He's got no taste for it. It will be wasted on him."

Auburn smiled. "Nonsense," she said. "Too much of the best is wasted on experience."

"I thought youth is wasted on the young," I said.

"That too," she said. "Let's make a trade. My best Scotch for a spot of your youth. Fair?"

"Fair," I said. She gave me the Scotch in a short heavy glass, with a generous helping of ice, and sat down across from us in the living room. After a few sips my shoulders sank into the plush cushions. I felt hot in the cheeks and loosened my tie. It was not a bad feeling. Looking at me, my father seemed to relax as well. Auburn coaxed him to talk about his coffee plantation in Vietnam, about the good life before the war. He talked until a buzzer went off in the kitchen, breaking him out of his reverie.

"That's dinner," Auburn said. "Let's move into the dining room."

Auburn had a maid who arranged the place settings. Dinner was served on silver platters beneath a crystal chandelier, reflecting both the rays of the setting sun and the klieg lights from the ski slopes of Grouse Mountain.

As big as the apartment was, the dining room was small and the table setting intimate. There was a *terrine rustique* for the entree, *coq au vin* for the main.

My father was not much of a drinker, but he lifted his glass merrily at the wine service. "I haven't had French food this good since Vietnam," my father said.

The more my father ate and drank the more his appetite grew, for both food and for conversation. At some point the topic of conversation turned to me. My father told her that I was an "A-plus-plus" student, a complete falsehood.

"He has a good mind for numbers," he said. Another complete falsehood. Math was my weakest subject. "I always tell my son that being good with numbers will give him keys in business. There are enough salesmen in the world. But having numbers is a key. Do you agree?"

"I absolutely agree," said Auburn. "You know, sometimes I do miss not having little ones of my own. Just a little."

"Children can be too much trouble sometimes," said my father. My father smiled at Auburn, as if I wasn't in the room. "I always tell my son that if he really wants to be a business-man, he has to fix his eyes. Any man can look into my son's eyes and tell what he is thinking."

"Well, he's young yet," said Auburn. She turned to me. "It must have been hard doing it all yourself."

My father looked deeply into his glass of red wine, almost empty. "I don't remember any other way," he said. In truth my father had always left me to my own devices. It took all I had to not tell Auburn as much.

After we finished the *coq au vin* the maid brought out a selection of cheeses. "You know," my father said, "there are roasting houses on every corner of Vancouver, but I never come in."

"Why not?" said Auburn.

"The smell. It is never fresh." My father rhapsodized about the smell of the coffee cherries on his plantation while they were still encased in their red skin and connected to the soil. How their scent changed from day to day. When it rained the whole plantation would smell like a field of mushrooms, on spring days wildflowers, on dry days cinnamon. My father believed that you can only judge the quality of coffee when the cherries are still alive and connected to the plant, when you can take the measure of the stalk and the soil with your stained fingers. The bean is the last of it. My father laughed at the people who whiffed adoringly at roasted beans. "It is like testing quality from the scent of cadavers," he said.

Auburn smiled while my father spoke, until dessert arrived. And after dessert was the main event. There was a bulge in the inside pocket of my father's blazer, where he kept the last of his "Vietnamese blend" in a brown paper bag. He handed the bag to Auburn. We followed her into the kitchen which, despite the clutter of hanging pans, seemed a vast and airy space. She ground the beans, not finely like my father would, but leaving the grounds with coarse edges. She had one white cup, in which she placed a large spoonful of the grounds. She boiled the water in a silver teapot, and poured water into the cup through the narrow spout.

We all stood there watching the cup in silence for what felt like an eternity, until an oak crust formed at the top. Then, as if merely to break the silence, Auburn took the cup to her nose, and cracked open the crust with the spoon. I stood behind her, took a deep breath, and was in the mountains of Vietnam. Then Auburn puckered her lips and slurped the cup loudly, swished coffee in her mouth, then spat it out into the kitchen sink.

"What's wrong with it?" said my father.

"Absolutely nothing," said Auburn, wiping her mouth, a drop of brown blood staining her lip. "It's beautiful."

We returned to the dining room and Auburn personally served us the rest of the coffee. We drank in silence. Then Auburn straightened up.

"We'll open a new world," she said. "Have you thought of terms?"

"Terms?" said my father.

Auburn smiled. "Terms," she repeated. "For a sub-brokerage contract."

"I should talk to my counterpart in Vietnam," he said. I had never heard my father say "counterpart" before.

Auburn looked at her watch. "It should be morning over the South China Sea." She had a teleconference facility in her office. My father got up from the table heavily. Each one of the rooms in Auburn's apartment struck a different tone. The grand airiness of the living room yielded to the dining room's dimly lit formality. But unlike the orderliness of the rest of the apartment, Auburn's office was a shamble of papers. She apologized for the mess. "It's the one room where I spend most of my time," she said.

On Auburn's wall and desk were colourful photos of her standing in the middle of coffee plantations throughout the world, in Brazil, in Africa, in Indonesia, sometimes with her hair tied back, sometimes loose and windswept.

"Who took these pictures?" asked my father.

"Usually the plantation owners," said Auburn. "My clients."

"And this one?" asked my father, pointing to another photo. She was in a canoe, holding an oar, a close-up to her young face, staring straight into the camera with a smile my father had never seen.

"My late husband," she said. "We weren't even married when this picture was taken."

The two lingered over the photos, circling them and each other.

Finally, Auburn said, "Do you have your counterpart's contact number?"

My father stammered. "I do," he said. "I didn't bring a phone card."

"That's fine," said Auburn. "We'll expense it."

We sat down around Auburn's desk. Mr Pham answered the phone with a bright and crisp "Hello," as if he was expecting us.

My father acted as a Vietnamese–English translator for Mr Pham and Auburn. They spoke of crop yields and currency fluctuations, about the lifted US embargo and holding corporations. My father controlled the conversation's pace and fluency. He did not merely translate but curated Mr Pham's words, burnishing their eloquence before passing his words along to Auburn.

I could see a fire smouldering as they discussed obstacles and stumbling blocks, like how much coffee were Auburn's clients really interested in buying, how soon could she get the commitments, who would cover the shipping costs?

Over the thousands of miles of fibre-optic cable I could hear Mr Pham muttering to himself about the shipping costs. He had not thought about that. "*Mon dieu,*" he muttered to himself.

"*Parlez-vous français?*" said Auburn.

"*Mais oui, bien sûr,*" said Mr Pham. "*Tous les Vietnamiens d'un certain âge parlent français.*"

"*C'est très bien,*" said Auburn. The conversation ended, to be continued soon. It was getting late here in Vancouver and in Vietnam Mr Pham had to attend to the appointments of his warming day.

The evening became liquid after that, both flowing and losing its shape. We finished with a nightcap in the living room. No one spoke of the conference call, of this partnership that was coming to life. Like youths making an intimate connection the night before, we all felt an inner glow that was fragile, a small candle flame that we didn't want to blow out with too much talk. We exchanged dull pleasantries and then Auburn called a cab to take us back home.

In the cab my father told me that I would be needing more summer suits, that we'd be flying back to Vietnam before too long, that we'd be speaking to Mr Pham, that my father would once again set foot on his coffee plantation. At home, I fell asleep even though my father had the TV on loud.

But Auburn did not come into my father's coffee shop the next evening, nor the next. He would not phone her though. Another week passed, and then in the week after he bought another phone card and phoned Mr Pham.

"I'm sorry about the delay," said my father. "Everything has been so busy here."

"I don't know what you mean," said Mr Pham. "We are arranging for a shipment of a tonne this spring."

"You've spoken to the woman?" said my father.

"Yes, she called. I've never spoken so much French all my life."

My father was silent.

"Will you be coming this summer?" said Mr Pham. Mr Pham said that Auburn would be coming to Vietnam in August to visit the plantation. "If you are, you'd better get a move on about visas."

"I'll have to look into it," said my father, and hung up. My father pulled out Auburn's business card and called her number several times, always getting a machine. He thought about phoning the police, but it was no longer his plantation. He was just the matchmaker. Around a year later my father walked into a Murchie's Tea & Coffee. There it was, on the display case, fair trade coffee from the mountains of Vietnam in a shiny plastic bag. He made me drink a cup with him at home. It tasted exactly as he remembered.

EVERYTHING TURNS AWAY

Steven Heighton

> About suffering they were never wrong,
> The Old Masters: how well they understood
> Its human position; how it takes place
> While someone else is eating or opening a window or just
> dully walking along
>
> — W. H. Auden,
>   "Musée des Beaux Arts"

I

The first of June 2015 was also the first day of ideal summery weather, hot but not humid, the grass and young leaves as freshly green as they would get, the banks of lilac along the old railway line in exuberant bloom. We were driving west into the franchise fringes of town in a silver Toyota Corolla that had rolled off the assembly line near the end of the previous century. We meant to test drive several less-used Toyotas at a dealership overlooking a postcard marina on a Lake Ontario bay.

A salesman named Walter—heavy, bespectacled, delivering his pitches in the laconic monotone of a man who has learned not to get his hopes up—introduced us to the three prospects

I'd found online. One was a new-looking black Prius hybrid that cost about five thousand dollars more than we were ready to pay. I'd thought I might be able to bargain, but Walter in his anaesthetized drawl apologized that in this case the price was final. Still, the crimson Camry was promising—the paint looked fresh, the odometer reading was modest, and the price was in our range. Walter handed me the key, slapped a magnetic test-drive licence plate into the slot above the rear fender, and off we drove. He sat beside me, raking his hand through an auburn comb-over that the wind kept compromising, while my wife, Mary, and seventeen-year-old daughter, Elena, sat in the back.

"Lovely day for a drive, isn't it, Steve," drawled Walter. In some retail circles, I guess, they still believe in punctuating every sentence with the target customer's name—a gambit that seems touchingly antiquated. Aren't we all too savvy nowadays for such obvious sales cons? But we're also lonelier and needier, so maybe charades of kindness and kinship still trigger a gratified response after all.

We, I write, as if there's a parity of loneliness between mere melancholics, like myself, and the catastrophically depressed. I've wondered if I have the right to frame this story—by which I mean, translate and shape such harrowing data.

Walter went on personalizing his sales script with *Steve*s as he directed me along what he called "test drive route numero uno." The route comprised urban and rural stretches and a drag strip of vacant highway where you could assess a car's acceleration; the Camry had a lot more pickup than our failing Corolla.

We were returning to the dealership the same way we'd set out, on a busy four-lane road that ran alongside the backyards of modest suburban houses from the '60s or '70s, their decks or patios visible some thirty metres away through the trees. It was along this stretch that I became aware, in spite of Walter's autopilot patter, that behind us Mary and Elena were anxiously discussing something.

Mary tapped me on the shoulder.

"Excuse me"—this more to Walter, who was talking—"I think we should pull over for a second."

I asked what was going on.

"We need to back up. Elena thinks something's wrong back there."

"With the car?" Walter asked with a resigned sigh.

"She thinks someone might be hurt."

I pulled over onto the gravel and stopped. Elena leaned forward as I turned to look back, her face serious, close to mine. She said, "I saw something the first time we went by, but that was from the far lane. I just saw again, closer. I think a guy is hurt, maybe unconscious."

I started to back up along the shoulder. Mary said, "She had to point him out to me. Maybe he was drunk and fell. He's lying on his deck. She says he hasn't moved since the first time we passed."

"I think he might be bleeding," Elena said.

"She thought he might be wearing a red cap."

"He's there, Dad!"

I stopped again. For the first time on our test drive, silence from Walter.

"His face is still upside down," Elena said. "His head's back over the edge."

"Probably sleeping one off," Walter said. "I can't see anything, but then I'm due for new specs."

"It's not a red cap," Elena said quietly.

I looked hard but couldn't see the man either, though I saw the deck, the patio doors, a white-brick bungalow. From my point of view the branch of a large tree beside the road was hiding part of the deck.

"Could be drugs, too," Walter said. "He'll probably be okay, though."

"He's not okay," Elena said.

I pulled back onto the road, U-turned, accelerated up the inner lane and veered left on a yellow light just as it turned red. Silence in the car—Walter rigid, his arms stretched straight in front of him, thick veinless hands braced on the dashboard. I drove a block west and turned south onto a quiet residential street.

"Here?"

"I think so," Elena said.

I pulled in at the curb in front of a landscaped front yard: groomed flower beds, hedges, a blue spruce symmetrical as an artificial Christmas tree. Beyond it, a white bungalow. Picture window, drapes drawn. The vacant driveway recently paved. As I jumped out Mary said, "Don't go behind the house yet— knock on the door."

"Why?"

"Could be a drug thing—there might be someone back there."

Walter was staring ahead through the windshield with unblinking eyes.

"Be careful, Dad!"

Elena's concern was touching and then disturbing as it hit me that she with her sharp vision had seen something we couldn't, something "not okay." I walked toward the house, my legs weightless with adrenaline. As always in situations of potential emergency I was excited; also worried about the fallen man; also anxious about seeming a busybody, puncturing a stranger's privacy, maybe antagonizing some hostile type whose friend or customer had passed out on the back deck.

I rapped on the solid door. From the other side, a detonation of high-pitched barking. The outburst subsided until I knocked again. I looked back at the car. Mary and Elena— faces side by side—watched me through the open back window. Walter too had now turned his pale, despairing face in my direction. I walked past the garage, rounded the corner, and ran along the concrete walk that led toward the backyard.

I emerged into the yard and froze. Ten feet away, a man was lying face up on the sunlit pine of the deck, his head lolling back over the edge as if craning to look across the yard toward the road. Because the deck was the height of my chest, he lay directly in front of me. A grey-green face under streaks and spatters of dried blood. The eyes shut hard. On his emaciated torso, as if placed there lengthwise, a polished mahogany cane. Cane, emaciated, old or ailing—he has slipped, fallen, smacked his head. Unconscious? No, it's too late. He's gone. I have never seen a body look so utterly vacated.

These impressions occupy maybe two or three seconds. I'm caught inside a coroner's forensic snapshot. No: it's not a finished image but a fresh print, still developing, the polished cane transforming into the stock of a rifle, no, something shorter, thicker, a shotgun fallen onto the man's torso. Barrel toward the face. The blood there not from facial wounds but splattered up from below. I can't see the wound, or somehow don't see it, and in fact I'm already turning and fleeing back toward the car. The passengers gape as I run toward them. I leap in, slam the door, start the car, and babble words at them, *old man, shotgun, suicide, dead.*

One reason to explore a horrific event in non-fictional instead of fictional terms is to avoid having to convince the reader of the plausibility of key details, no matter how far-fetched. It is 2015. In a speeding vehicle sit three middle-aged adults, one of them a used-car salesman. A teenager sits with them. And not one of these four individuals is carrying a phone. My daughter has left hers in our car in the parking lot at the dealership. Walter has always seen these drives as a chance to get away from calls, he explains now—adding softly, hopelessly, as if assuming I'll ignore him, "Better not speed, Steve . . .

We're almost there ... If he passed a while ago, a minute won't matter."

Silence from the back seat. I look in the rear-view mirror: Elena staring fixedly out her window. We reach the dealership a few minutes later. Mary and Elena decide to wait outside in the parking lot while Walter leads me in through the show-room to his open-concept cubicle. It's like the mock-up of an office on a stage: three walls that go partway to the ceiling, no front wall at all. He gestures toward his chair, his desk, an office phone. I sit and key in 911. I try to speak calmly, quickly. A burning current crawls under my scalp. The pulse in my jaw is like a second heartbeat. The dispatcher, as if new to the job or too sensitive for it, sounds genuinely shaken.

"I wonder if I should have stayed with him," I say, feeling queasier as it hits me: by leaving the scene I might have done something unconscionable. The body is alone, as it must have been for who knows how long before we arrived, and this condition—of almost interstellar solitude—is a terrible insult and indignity.

"No," the dispatcher tells me. "There was a gun there, you had to leave."

She gets me to repeat the address, sends two police cars and an ambulance, then keeps me on the line to collect my own details—address, telephone number—as well as Walter's. He's leaning against the back hatch of a gleaming charcoal-grey SUV, polishing the lenses of his glasses with a Kleenex, as I recite coordinates into the phone.

I hang up and stare at my hand, still gripping the receiver. The hand looks prosthetic. My wristwatch says 12:16. I half see Walter approaching his desk, approaching me, this stran-ger in his chair. He leans down and—as if gently reminding me of the masculine duty to push on with life's errands in the face of disaster—murmurs, "Dare I ask, Steve, if you've made a decision about the Camry?"

Two hours later a cop parked his motorcycle in front of our house. I led him around to the side porch and we sat down. He drank strong-smelling coffee out of a stainless-steel mug he'd brought, while I tried to sip a beer that I wanted to guzzle. I wanted something stiffer than beer but wondered if I was already violating some statute by drinking while providing a sworn statement. The man was messily printing my account on foolscap with a pencil. I tried to describe exactly what I'd seen and done—often a challenge for a fiction writer, although not in this case. The incident seemed—still seems—to deny any licence to the part of me that compulsively reshapes or redacts experiences.

The cop was tall, had an action-figure physique, and wore aviator shades and motorcycle boots. Despite the glare he removed his sunglasses, exposing thoughtful blue eyes and long lashes.

"Such a beautiful day, too," I said moronically.

"Those tend to be the worst ones," he said. "It's a myth that Christmas is the worst time."

Still buzzing, hardly able to sit still, I blurted that maybe the first true summer day feels like a leering "fuck you" to someone whose inner world is gripped in winter. The cop inclined his head noncommittally. After a moment he said he hadn't gone into the backyard with the paramedics—he didn't need to see that sort of thing, he'd seen one too many.

I asked about the dead man and, a little to my surprise, the cop related as much as he knew—not much, but enough to collapse my assumptions and deductions. The victim was not old, just in his late fifties. He didn't live alone, although on the morning of his death he was alone, except for that dog I'd heard barking.

"We're trying to track down his wife. Looks like she went out of town for the weekend."

"So he planned this—waited for her to leave," I said, instantly replacing my old assumptions with new ones. *She was with another man and didn't realize he knew.* Or, *There was no other man, but she was leaving him anyway.*

"And he recently retired from the military," the cop said.

"Could he have been over in Afghanistan?" I asked, then added, "No. Probably too old."

Was I making the cop uneasy? Likely he was unused to such persistent curiosity and reflexive deduction—the professional habits of fiction writers and investigative journalists, along with private detectives, gossips and conspiracy theorists.

I told the cop how surprised I was that no one had seen or heard a thing. He explained that one neighbour did hear something, around 10:00 a.m., but figured it was a big firecracker.

"So he was lying there for two hours."

"I'm afraid so."

The cop gave me contact details for mental health professionals that we, and especially Elena, might want to consult. As he got to his feet he said, "You should be proud of your daughter. Good eyes." He pointed to his own eyes as he slid his sunglasses back on. "And she chose to speak up."

The realization that your child is further evolved than you were at her age both humbles you and makes you proud; that she's conscientious, empathetic, an adult in a world understaffed by adults. All that. But she will have to carry something heavier than you ever did at seventeen, something that might linger for years on the threshold of her sleeps.

II

For ten mornings afterward, I checked the obituaries on the website of the local newspaper until I found it. I didn't recognize the face in the overexposed black-and-white photo; it looked much fuller and younger than the blood-streaked face I'd glimpsed. But other details made me all but certain:

the date of death, the code phrase "died suddenly" and a reference to retirement from a logistical job in the military. An
online check to link the surname to the house address came
up positive: a paving company listed his driveway as a recent
contract.

I made a note of the memorial service date.

From the beginning I'd felt that if there was a service, and
if I found the information in time, I should try to attend. Again
forming an assumption out of skimpy evidence and ready
stereotypes, I'd decided that few mourners would be present. A
final existential insult. The military, I guessed, might dispatch
some kind of small delegation, but who could say? Elena told
me she thought she might want to attend as well. Our intention
was to enter quietly, sit at the back, and slip out before any next
of kin could approach and ask about our connection with the
deceased.

On the morning of the memorial service, she decided not to
go. I didn't ask her to explain her decision. I put on some decent
clothes but then, agonizing, changed back into my summer
writing gear—cargo shorts and a T-shirt—before deciding last
minute that I had to go after all. I dressed again and ran out the
front door, re-knotting my tie as I jogged the five blocks to the
funeral home chapel.

Sitting at the back turned out to be the only option. At
least two hundred people, dozens of them in military dress
uniform, packed the room. There were children; there were
teenagers who looked genuinely distraught, not simply drag-
ooned into the pews. My sense of relief was twofold: people
had come to mourn the man after all and, for that very reason,
I could come and go anonymously.

The widow, barely able to walk, was helped up the aisle
by bulky men who looked awkward in ill-fitting suits and
loose-knotted ties. Over the next hour she remained seated
and sobbing at the front, while others got up to speak at the
lectern. Then a priest with a bald head, a boyish face and an

irrepressibly sunny demeanour read a eulogy the widow had written. The content and tone made it clear that the manner of the man's death was no secret. In his late forties he had slid into depression and then, developing ailments unspecified in the eulogy, had to give up or cut back on the physical outlets that had helped him manage: beer league baseball, fly fishing and, more recently and devotedly, gardening. Now it came back to me: the landscaped front yard, the trimmed hedges, the parterred and graded flower beds that—come to think of it—had been sparsely flowered despite the season. Maybe just perennials, the stubborn aftermath of his endeavour.

In the room where I write, I unshelve a plump, important-looking anthology and turn to the poem "Musée des Beaux Arts," in which W. H. Auden reflects on Pieter Brueghel the Elder's painting *Landscape with the Fall of Icarus*:

> how everything turns away
> Quite leisurely from the disaster; the ploughman may
> Have heard the splash, the forsaken cry,
> But for him it was not an important failure; the sun shone
> As it had to on the white legs disappearing into the green
> Water

In a footnote, the anthologists observe that the figures in Brueghel's composition have not only failed to notice Icarus plunging out of the sky but also "a dead body in the woods." I quickly find a reproduction of the painting online. Locating the overlooked body is less easy, but eventually—using the magnifying tool to search the woods beyond a field that a farmer and his horse are plowing—I spot him. Only his face shows clearly, inverted, staring upward, white against the dark forest floor. I recoil from the screen; his positioning and pallor strongly recall the face of the man on the deck.

Could Auden have missed the figure? He wrote his poem after examining the painting in the Musées royaux des Beaux-Arts in Brussels and he must have studied the work closely. I assume he saw but chose to ignore that secondary, nameless casualty and to focus on Icarus. If so, it was the right decision. Adding a stanza of reflections on the dead stranger would have herniated the poem, introducing a distracting sidebar, like dropping a second protagonist into a short story.

But visual art works differently, and the face in the woods is integral to the painting. On one level, it serves as a memento mori, one of those small skulls that Renaissance artists planted in the margins of their works as quiet reminders of mortality. And because of its placement on the left side of the canvas, the head also serves as a compositional balance to Icarus, who is plunging into the sea on the lower right side. The balancing works anatomically as well: the dead man's face, along with a bit of his dark-clad torso blending into the undergrowth, physically completes Icarus, of whom we see only a pair of white legs.

Each one's unwitnessed fate echoes the other's, yet the hidden victim seems so much more forlorn. Icarus, after all, is the namesake of the painting, the title of which will direct any viewer to search out and find his submerging form. Nor is Icarus hard to find: his legs, in contrast to the gloomily shaded face in the woods, are lit up by the setting sun. Above all, Icarus is an illustrious figure—a sort of misbehaving celebrity, a universal metaphor, a byword to the point of cliché.

At the chapel the jaunty priest, still failing to funeralize his demeanour, read from Psalm 34: *The Lord is close to the broken-hearted. He rescues those whose spirits are crushed.*

A sense of being unseen, alone and spectral, must be a root sorrow for many of the broken; yet there's more than one way of not being seen. You can feel insignificant to the point of invisibility or—while living an outwardly successful,

hence *visible*, life—sink under the weight of a pain unappar-
ent to the world.

Maybe Icarus, that golden boy, was a suicide too.

As for the ones who feel invisible suicide may simply final-
ize a self-perceived erasure. Maybe these few thousand words
are all trying to say the same thing: you were seen, hence a
little less alone, during the two hours after your death.

At home I studied the program from the service. The photo
on the front showed a man in his late twenties or early thirties,
lanky, fit in the implicit manner of people who work physically but don't frequent weight rooms. His stance: confident
but not cocky. Relaxed grin. He's wearing a white T-shirt half-
tucked into faded jeans, and a red baseball cap, like the one
Elena first thought he might have on. Behind him, a chain-
link backstop and beyond that a baseball diamond. Judging
by the light and the state of the outfield grass, it's late spring.

I'd set him in motion on that ripening field, loping and
tossing the ball to friends, fielding grounders with that easy-
going grin, or wincing into the sun as he tracks a pop fly I've
hit out to him. Later, we return to the bleachers and gather
around a Styrofoam cooler packed with squat, iodine-brown
bottles of Brador that he and his friends snap open with their
lighters. Little older than my daughter is now, I barely say a
word, shyly thrilled to be present, swigging beer, humoured
by men who are firmly at home in their adult lives.

Trying to finish this piece—trying to pin down, after my various
misconstructions, whatever was solidly knowable—I decided
to compare my recall of his home and neighbourhood to the
reality. But I couldn't drive out there; our Corolla was back in
the shop. So I turned to Google Street View.

In that eerily paused, preserved little world the sun was
high, the trees in bud but not yet in leaf—that equivocal pre-
season in Kingston when the light, unfiltered by greenery, is

dazzling, yet the winds off the lake remain wintry. I clicked on a link and found a date for the images: mid-April, just over a year before the suicide.

I began on the main road from which Elena first glimpsed him, but I couldn't tell which backyard was his. I navigated round to his own street. Again, nothing looked right. I checked my notes for his address, then left-clicked back up the street in blurring little surges.

Finally I recognized the house. The blue spruce looked more familiar by the moment, as did the fieldstone half fence that I only now recalled, and those terraced garden beds raked and ready for the spring flowers. In the foreground at the bottom of the driveway sat a phalanx of brown-paper yard waste bags, evenly packed to the top, and behind them a bundle of neatly tied deadfall and trimmed branches. I glided ghostlike back down the street: no one else had left anything out for collection. Did the neighbours not bother with their yards or had the man always tidied up and then set out his refuse early in the season, ahead of collection day?

Gardening is a promissory, optimistic act. To sow is to project, to cast your faith forward into the next season or the following spring. Stumbling on this evidence of his diligence and care—this generative intention still active just a few hundred days before he blew out his heart—moved me very much.

Now I imagine the Street View vehicle, with its mounted camera, passing along the main road not when it did but some thirteen months later, the beautiful morning of his death. If I and Walter, among hundreds or thousands of others, had missed his face amid the branches and shadows of his backyard, then the Street View curators who screen the panoramas for legal reasons might have missed him too. Certainly they would have missed him. The image would still be saved online, his face half-hidden in the landscape.

METCALF-ROOKE AWARD 2023

We have always considered the very best short stories to be closer to poetry and song than to the meat-and-potatoes of everyday prose. We want the music of short stories to lift us from this world to theirs. There is no prescription for such writing. It is not a trick or a technical device. It is a gift that language bestows.

From her earliest stories in *Bad Imaginings* to her most recent in *Ellen in Pieces*, Caroline Adderson has served language and song with brilliance and we are delighted to further honour her.

John Metcalf, Ottawa
Leon Rooke, Toronto

CONTRIBUTORS' BIOGRAPHIES

Caroline Adderson is the author of five novels (*A History of Forgetting, Sitting Practice, The Sky Is Falling, Ellen in Pieces, A Russian Sister*) and two collections of short stories (*Bad Imaginings, Pleased to Meet You*) as well as many books for young readers. She is also the editor and co-contributor of a non-fiction book of essays and photographs, *Vancouver Vanishes: Narratives of Demolition and Revival,* and guest editor of *Best Canadian Stories 2019.* Her work has received numerous award nominations including the *Sunday Times* EFG Private Bank Short Story Award, the International IMPAC Dublin Literary Award, two Commonwealth Writers' Prizes, the Governor General's Literary Award, the Rogers Writers' Trust Fiction Prize, and the Scotiabank Giller Prize longlist. In 2017, she was a nominee for the YWCA Women of Distinction Award for Arts, Culture and Design. Her awards include three BC Book Prizes, three CBC Literary Awards, the Marian Engel Award for mid-career achievement, and a National Magazine Award Gold Medal for Fiction. She teaches in the Writing and Publishing Program at SFU and is the Program Director of the Writing Studio at the Banff Centre for Arts and Creativity.

www.carolineadderson.com

David Bezmozgis is the author of the story collections *Immigrant City* and *Natasha and Other Stories*, and the novels *The Betrayers* and *The Free World*.

David's stories have appeared in numerous publications including *The New Yorker, Harpers, Zoetrope All-Story*, and *The Walrus* and have twice been included in *The Best American Short Stories*.

His books have been nominated for the Scotiabank Giller Prize, the Governor General's Award, and the Trillium Prize. He has won the Amazon.ca First Novel Award and the National Jewish Book Award.

A graduate of the University of Southern California's School of Cinematic Arts, David's first feature film, *Victoria Day*, premiered in competition at the Sundance Film Festival. His second feature was an adaptation of his story "Natasha." Most recently, he was a screenwriter on the animated feature film *Charlotte*, about the life of the German-Jewish artist Charlotte Salomon.

Born in Riga, Latvia, David lives in Toronto where he is the Creative Director of the Humber School for Writers.

Jowita Bydlowska is the author of *Drunk Mom* and *Guy*. She immigrated to Canada as a teenager. Her new novel, *Possessed*, comes out in October 2022.

Kate Cayley has published two short story collections, *How You Were Born* and *Householders*, and two collections of poetry, *When This World Comes to an End* and *Other Houses*. Her plays have been performed in Canada, the US, and the UK. She has won the Trillium Book Award, an O. Henry Prize, and the Mitchell Prize for Poetry, and has been a finalist for the Governor General's Literary Award for Fiction and the K. M. Hunter Award. She is a frequent writing collaborator with immersive company Zuppa Theatre, and has been a writer-in-residence with Tarragon Theatre, McMaster University, and the Toronto Public Library. Her third collection of poems, *Lent*, is forthcoming from Book*hug. She lives in Toronto with her wife and their three children.

Tamas Dobozy is a professor in the Department of English and Film Studies at Wilfrid Laurier University. He lives in Kitchener, Ontario. He has published four books of short fiction, *When X Equals Marylou*, *Last Notes and Other Stories*, *Siege 13: Stories* (which won the 2012 Rogers Writers' Trust Fiction Prize, and was shortlisted for both the Governor General's Literary Award for Fiction, and the 2013 Frank O'Connor International Short Story Award), and most recently, *Ghost Geographies: Fictions*. He has published over seventy short stories in journals such as *One Story*, *Fiction*, *Agni*, and *Granta*, and won an O. Henry Prize in 2011, and the Gold Medal for Fiction at the National Magazine Awards in 2014.

Omar El Akkad is an author and journalist. He was born in Egypt, grew up in Qatar, moved to Canada as a teenager, and now lives in the United States. The start of his journalism career coincided with the start of the war on terror, and over the following decade he reported from Afghanistan, Guantánamo Bay, and many other locations around the world. His work earned a National Newspaper Award for Investigative Journalism and the Goff Penny Award for young journalists. His fiction and non-fiction writing has appeared in *The New York Times*, *The Guardian*, *Le Monde*, *Guernica*, *GQ*, and many other newspapers and magazines. His debut novel, *American War*, is an international bestseller and has been translated into thirteen languages. It won the Pacific Northwest Booksellers' Award, the Oregon Book Award for fiction, and the Kobo Emerging Writer Prize and has been nominated for more than ten other awards. It was listed as one of the best books of the year by *The New York Times*, *The Washington Post*, *GQ*, NPR, and *Esquire* and was selected by the BBC as one of 100 novels that changed our world. His latest novel, *What Strange Paradise*, was released in July 2021 and won the Scotiabank Giller Prize, the Pacific Northwest Booksellers' Award, the Oregon Book Award for fiction, and was shortlisted for the Aspen Words Literary Prize. It was also named a best book of the year by *The New York Times*, *The Washington Post*, NPR, and several other publications.

Christine Estima's essays and short stories have appeared in *The New York Times*, *The Observer*, *The Walrus*, *New York Daily News*, *VICE*, *The Globe and Mail*, the *Toronto Star*, CBC, etalk, *Bitch Magazine*, *Maisonneuve*, *PRISM International*, *The Malahat Review*, *The New Quarterly*, *The Antigonish Review*, *Prairie Fire*, *Descant*, *Grain*, *Event*, *Broken Pencil*, *Subterrain*, *Matrix Magazine*, *The Puritan*, *Notre Dame Review*, and many more. She was shortlisted for the 2018 Allan Slaight Prize for Journalism, longlisted for the 2015 CBC Canada Writes Creative Nonfiction prize, and was a finalist in the 2011 Writers' Union of Canada short prose competition. Please visit ChristineEstima.com for more.

Born in 1987 in Uashat, an Innu community near Sept-Îles, **Naomi Fontaine** is a French teacher who graduated from Laval University. This is where her writerly talents were noticed by François Bon, her creative writing professor.

Convinced that her unique voice should be read and heard, he encouraged her creative process. In 2011, she published her first novel, *Kuessipan* (Mémoire d'encrier), which was greatly successful and earned her a mention for the Prix des Cinq Continents de la Francophonie.

She returned to Uashat to begin her teaching in her community. Her students inspired her second novel, *Manikanetish* (Mémoire d'encrier, 2017), where she portrays them with pride so that they too can see all the perseverance they show.

Her work has been published in various journals, collectives, and online.

Named one of the "women of the year" by *Elle Québec* in 2011, Naomi Fontaine wishes to put the nature of human beings and their courage in the foreground.

Attached to her people, she writes the visions of the Innu, what their eyes have experienced. She considers that the Innu have too often been described as a statistic. For her, you must show it as it is and escape stereotypes.

Shuni is her most recent novel.

Sara Freeman is a Montreal-born, Boston-based writer. Her writing has appeared in *The Sewanee Review*, *Granta*, and *Joyland*, among others. Her debut novel is *Tides*.

Steven Heighton (1961–2022) was the author of nineteen books, including the Writers' Trust Hilary Weston Prize finalist *Reaching Mithymna: Among the Volunteers and Refugees on Lesvos* and *The Waking Comes Late*, winner of the Governor General's Literary Award for Poetry.

A settler writer, educator, and critic from Kjipuktuk (Halifax), **David Huebert** (he/him) teaches literature and creative writing at the University of New Brunswick. David's fiction debut, *Peninsula Sinking*, won a Dartmouth Book Award and was runner-up for the Danuta Gleed Literary Award. His latest book, *Chemical Valley* (Biblioasis 2021), won the Alistair MacLeod Prize for Short Fiction and was shortlisted for the Thomas Raddall Atlantic Fiction Award. David lives in Fredericton with his partner and children and a fluffy white cat named Moby Dick.

Philip Huynh's collection of short stories, *The Forbidden Purple City*, was published in 2019 (Goose Lane Editions) and was a finalist for the City of Vancouver Book Award and the George

Ryga Award for Social Awareness in Literature. A manuscript of the collection was the co-winner of the Jim Wong-Chu Emerging Writers Award. His fiction has been published in numerous literary journals and two editions of the *Journey Prize* anthology, and cited for distinction in *The Best American Stories*. A graduate of the University of British Columbia, Huynh is also a practising lawyer. He lives in Richmond, BC, with his wife and twin daughters.

Alexandra Mae Jones is a queer writer based in Toronto and the author of the young adult novel *The Queen of Junk Island*, which came out with Annick Press in 2022. Her short fiction has appeared in publications including *Third Wednesday*, *Frond Literary*, and *EVENT*, and she won first prize in *Prairie Fire*'s 2020 fiction contest. She has an MFA in creative writing from the University of Guelph, and is a freelance reporter currently writing for CTVNews.ca. In her spare time, she paints, knits, crochets, and sometimes plays the ukulele poorly. *The Queen of Junk Island* is her first novel.

Kathryn Gabinet-Kroo was born and raised in Oregon, and after earning a BA from Cornell University, she moved to Canada, where she has been a professional artist for over forty years. She taught painting and drawing at the Saidye Bronfman Centre's School of Fine Arts for ten years. In 2001, she earned a master's in translation studies from Concordia University and since then has been working "both jobs" from her studio on the Lachine Canal. As a freelance translator, she has worked for clients in the public and private sector including, among others, the Canada Council for the Arts, the Museum of Civilization, Fisheries and Oceans Canada, Environment Canada, and the Courts Administration Service. Her true passion is literary translation, and her translations of nine novels and short story collections have been published. Translations of shorter works and excerpts have appeared in print and online media as well. She specializes in contemporary Quebec literature and in works by Indigenous writers in particular. Kathryn is a member of the Literary Translators Association of Canada (LTAC) and the Quebec Writers' Federation (QWF).

Carmelinda Scian won the *Malahat Review* Open Season Award (2013), the *Toronto Star*'s short story contest (2015), and a Disquiet Scholarship (2019). She participated in the 2018 International Conference on the Short Story in English (theme: Beyond History—the Radiance of the Short Story), in Lisbon, and has been published in *Litro, Belletrist, Prairie Fire, The Fiddlehead,* the *San Antonio Review, Magnolia, The Antigonish Review, The Hong Kong Review*, and other literary journals. "Yellow Watch" was nominated for the 2018 Journey Prize. Her first novel, *Yellow Watch, Journey of a Portuguese Woman*, was published by Mawenzi House in Toronto in August 2022.

She was born in Algarve, Portugal, and immigrated to Canada with her family. She lives in Toronto.

MAGAZINES CONSULTED FOR THE 2023 EDITION

For the 2023 edition of *Best Canadian Stories*, the following publications were consulted:

Brick, Broken City, Broken Pencil, Canadian Notes & Queries, Carte Blanche, Catapult, The Dalhousie Review, Electric Literature, EVENT, Exile Quarterly, The Fiddlehead, filling Station, Freefall, Geist, Grain, Granta, Hazlitt, The Hong Kong Review, The Humber Literary Review, Hypertext Magazine, Jewish Fiction.net, Joyland, Maisonneuve, The Malahat Review, Maple Tree Literary Supplement, The Massachussets Review, Minola Review, Narrative Magazine, The Nashwaak Review, The New Quarterly, paperplates, The Paris Review, Plenitude, Prairie Fire, PRISM International, Pulp Literature, The Puritan, The Quarantine Review, Queen's Quarterly, Qwerty Magazine, Room, subTerrain, Taddle Creek, The /temz/ Review, THIS Magazine, The Threepenny Review, Uncanny Magazine, Understorey Magazine, The Walrus, The Windsor Review, WordCity Literary Journal, Zoetrope

ACKNOWLEDGEMENTS

"Instructions for the Drowning" by Steven Heighton first appeared in *The Threepenny Review*. Reprinted with permission of the estate.

"All Our Auld Acquaintances Are Gone" by Caroline Adderson first appeared in *Canadian Notes & Queries*. Reprinted with permission of the author.

"How to Fake a Breakdown" by Alexandra Mae Jones first appeared in *EVENT*. Reprinted with permission of the author.

"Palais Royale" by Tamas Dobozy first appeared in *The Fiddlehead*. Reprinted with permission of the author.

"A Death" by Kate Cayley first appeared in *The Fiddlehead*. Reprinted with permission of the author.

"Neka" by Naomi Fontaine and translated by Kathryn Gabinet-Kroo first appeared in *Exile Quarterly* and was published in *Amun* (Exile Editions, 2020). Reprinted with permission of the author, translator, and publisher.

ACKNOWLEDGEMENTS

"The Test" by David Bezmozgis first appeared in *Zoetrope*. Reprinted with permission of the author.

"Oddsmaking" by Omar El Akkad first appeared in *The Massachusetts Review*. Reprinted with permission of the author.

"Mother" by Jowita Bydlowska first appeared in *The Fiddlehead*. Reprinted with permission of the author.

"Your Hands Are Blessed" by Christine Estima first appeared in *Prairie Fire*. Reprinted with permission of the author.

"River Crossings" by Carmelinda Scian first appeared in *The Hong Kong Review* and was published in *Yellow Watch* (Mawenzi House, 2022). Reprinted with permission of the author and publisher.

"Oil People" by David Huebert first appeared in *Maisonneuve*. Reprinted with permission of the author.

"Tides" by Sara Freeman first appeared in *Granta* and was published in *Tides* (Hamish Hamilton, 2022). Reprinted with permission of the author and publisher.

"Doi Moi Beans" by Philip Huynh first appeared in *The Malahat Review*. Reprinted with permission of the author.

"Everything Turns Away" by Steven Heighton first appeared in *Geist*. Reprinted with permission of the estate.

ABOUT THE EDITOR

Mark Anthony Jarman is the author of *Touch Anywhere to Begin*, *Czech Techno*, *Knife Party at the Hotel Europa*, *19 Knives*, and the travel book *Ireland's Eye*. He has published fiction and creative non-fiction in Europe, India, Hong Kong, and North America. Jarman is a graduate of the Iowa Writers' Workshop and a fiction editor for *The Fiddlehead* literary journal in Canada.